REMEMBER *Us*

LOVE ENDURES • BOOK THREE

SUSAN WARNER

Published by EG Publishing, 2020
First Edition. January 22, 2020

REMEMBER *Us*

One

Michael Thalman had faced militia while defending architectural wonders. He'd faced twenty-foot long alligators to see buried cities under the water. He'd even done free soloing to get to an archeological site on a cliff, but all of that paled next to him going into this cabin and facing his estranged wife, Cora.

Cora was a powerhouse in her own right. She had a logical mind that was like a steel trap. It was that logic that had put them both in this situation. It was ironic and tragic all at once. They both owned Thalman Designs. Unfortunately, she had taken a leave from the company. Then she had taken a leave from him by moving out of their house. A year later, he had received papers from a lawyer saying she wanted a divorce.

That was when Michael realized he had been wrong to listen to everyone. After Cora and Michael had suffered a loss, Cora had withdrawn from him and their marriage. Everyone told him to give her time. It went against everything he felt, but he listened, and now here he was about to do something so extreme it gave even him pause.

Michael took a deep breath and tried not to let the overcast day bring him down. The plan had been so simple. Every year he came to Second Chances Camp to help foster kids' experience life outdoors. Recently, a friend of his, Christopher Griggs, was in the position to give his ticket to Cora. Michael thought if he could get Cora at the camp, they'd spend time remembering that they loved each other, and then they'd get back together. Well, maybe not that easy, but it would be a chance. Now that the moment was at hand, the only thought going through his head was, *this was the worst plan ever.*

The cabins were arranged in semi-circles, and Cora's cabin was in the Peppermint Circle. All of the circles led to the main road, and on that main road was the owner cabin and two other cabins. Michael knocked on the cabin door. Cora opened the door, and there was light in his life again. At first, she had that small smile that said welcome to everyone. Her dark hair was pulled back into a thick ponytail, and her cat shaped eyes were bright and inquisitive with long spiky lashes.

In the very next moments, however, her smile disappeared, and her blue eyes became cold and devoid of expression. Her demeanor changed, and once again, he was looking at the Cora she had become instead of the Cora he knew lurked within.

"Have you brought the papers?" she asked.

"No, I haven't."

For a moment, she looked confused, and one of her eyebrows raised as she waited for him to explain. Michael thought about not saying anything just to get her to speak again. All of their communications went through email. It had been a while since he had heard her husky tones. Hearing her voice brought back days of laughter and joy that had been fluttering on the fringes of his memory.

"So, you're probably wondering what I'm doing here?" he said as he leaned against the door.

"I'm wondering what you're doing here without papers in your hand."

"Well, I received the papers, and I made a decision," he said as the moment of truth was approaching, his nervousness was growing. Was it time apart that made him feel like a fish out of water?

If he were honest, he'd admit it was just Cora. Cora could make him unsure about his own name. She wrecked his senses with her femininity and confidence. She was his other half on so many levels, but it was hard to speak to her with this distance between them. She was his shelter, and now the doors had been shut to a place he thought he would always be welcome.

Michael needed her, it was that simple. There wasn't going to be a future for him without Cora. Michael stood six feet tall, so he had to make sure he didn't hover over Cora. She hated it when people got too close or loomed over her. Leaning against the doorframe gave him a moment to take in her appearance. She must have been working out or cleaning. It's the only time he had ever seen Cora in the gear she had on now. Grey sweat pants, a hot pink workout shirt, and black rubber-soled sneakers she looked like a fitness instructor you'd see doing those YouTube videos.

"I came to offer you a deal."

"You're late. I already sent mine," Cora stated.

"I think mine is more equitable than what was offered."

"I'm surprised, Michael. I never thought you'd go after the money, but I guess we all change."

Michael kept his smile pasted on his face as he took the verbal blow. "The old Michael would have jumped at that. No, I'm not here for money. I'm here for something way more valuable."

"Really?" Cora shifted her weight and locked her eyes with his.

"I'm here for you, Cora."

"Excuse me?"

Michael smiled. Cora was clearly confused, and she had taken a step back as if she were trying to understand where this was going. That spark was in her blue eyes. It was the twinkle of interest that came when she thought there was a mystery afoot or something she didn't understand.

"I saw your papers and then decided that we needed to work things out. So for the next couple of weeks, we are both here at the camp. I thought we'd—"

Cora shook her head and gifted him a grin. "Michael, that is the worst plan ever, even for you."

Michael let out a breath and shrugged. He was feeling foolish, but that grin made it all worth it. He only needed a little bit of hope, and there it was. His Cora was still in there. He had made it this far, he might as well go for the gold.

"The cabins are equipped with two rooms. I've been assigned to be your roomie and—"

"No."

"The camp is full of people to help the kids, and the other cabins are—"

"Well, it's a good thing you have been blessed with an inordinate amount of charm. There are a lot of things I'll do at this camp, but being your roomie won't be one of them."

"Cora, let's talk."

"Do you want to sign the divorce papers first? I'll let you in then."

Michael looked at her and was speechless. Cora shook her head.

"Somethings never change. You never even thought I'd let you stay in exchange for the papers. I—"

"Come in, this shouldn't take long for us to clear up," Cora said. She stepped aside, and Michael walked in. He took a breath, and he was breathing in Cora everywhere. She didn't wear loud perfumes, but she did buy a French soap that had a subtle aroma that he associated with Cora. She showed him to the sofa inside.

"Have a seat." Cora sat across from him. The room looked similar to the other rooms he'd seen in the cabins. Cora sat in the chair across from him.

"Cora, I think—"

She held up her hand. "I know you, Michael. You think that love conquers all. You think this is romantic. You think fighting for your true love is a life goal. You are an amazing, passionate man and a gifted architect, but you need to accept that love doesn't conquer all. If it were true, our baby would be here today. You've put a lot of effort into getting this meeting. Say your piece, and then you can go on with your life, and I can go on with mine."

Michael felt like the wind had been knocked out of him. Her words were stronger than any gut punch he'd received in real life, and the pain was as raw as an open wound.

"You're right. I came here with a plan that is going nothing like I thought it would. I came here for us and for our baby."

Cora's body stiffened in the chair, and only the whitening of her clasped hands in her lap gave Michael any clue that his words had any effect. "Be careful, Michael. I'd like to think we can still be civil to one another."

"We had a tragic loss, Cora. The truth of it is neither one of us are going on with our lives at all. You are working yourself day and night at your business, which is doing extremely well. I'm working at Thalman Designs, but it's not the same."

"Nothing is the same, Michael."

"Some things have changed, but others…not so much. Cora, I'm here because I love you. I'm here because you're right, I don't believe what we have is over. I'm here because when I dream of being old and holding a hand, it's yours. I know you don't see it, but I do. So here is my deal. While we're here at the camp give me a chance. A chance for you to remember us. Afterward, if you still feel the same way you do now, I'll sign the divorce papers."

He waited, watching emotions fly across her face. It would be decided here and now.

"You're not staying here, in this cabin with me."

"Done." He stood up and went to the door. Michael didn't wait for her to see him out. Instead, he went to the door and opened it. The sun shone outside, and he took a deep breath. It wasn't everything he wanted, but it was enough. It was a chance. She hadn't said no. Cora hadn't said yes either but she hadn't taken away all of his hope.

"Michael?"

Her voice was low. In fact, if she had waited a few more moments, he wouldn't have been able to hear her as he stood at the door. He didn't turn back. He didn't even want to breathe. Would this be the moment? Would she rip the rug of hope from beneath his feet?

"Yes?"

"I don't think it'll make a difference, but I'll try."

Michael nodded and went out the door. He had a smile on his face and a pep in his step. He wasn't sure where he was going to sleep tonight, but that didn't matter as much as Cora deciding to give him a chance.

Cora didn't turn when she heard the door close. She waited a few moments and then let out a breath.

"That man," Cora whispered to the room. *He's still the same emotional man he's always been. Who does this kind of madness anyway? I should have known it was too good to be true when Gina asked me to go away to a camp.*

She folded her hands and looked at her ring finger. The skin on her finger was lighter where her wedding ring used to be. Cora shook her head. She was just as mad as Michael. She'd just taken her wedding ring off as of two weeks ago. Who did that? Who sent papers asking for a divorce and still wore a ring?

Cora stood up and looked around the cabin. She was lonely. She missed the silly way Michael would do impersonations of the muppets to cheer her up. She missed watching television and having debates on issues. She should have told him yes to staying in the second bedroom, but when she saw him, she saw their little girl, Hope.

When Gina, a co-worker, approached her, she was cautious to help fill in, but Cora wanted to be a part of helping Gina and her happiness. After being separated for a year Gina had managed to reconcile with her true love, Christopher Griggs. As a favor, Gina had asked if Cora would attend the camp for her. After waiting a week of turning it over in her mind, Cora finally agreed to attend. Cora had thought Gina was a little passionate, but now that she was here, she could see the passion was probably coming from Michael.

Michael. Not even time could dull Michael. He was the man who sat down, looked at a goal, and went after it. It was how they met. He saw her on the street, and the next day he met her at the hot dog stand she went to for pretzels. And he brought a rose. She had been working as a project manager on a large account and was debating if that was all there was going to be in her life, working for someone else.

Then Michael happened. It went from meeting him at the hot dog stand, bringing a flower a day to her, and telling her something about herself that he really admired.

She had tried to dissuade him. After the flowers had stopped, she waited for the pickup line that would ask for more than what she was ready to give. Instead, the next day he showed up at the stand, and he said, "I'd like us to get to know each other better. So for every time I say something about you that is correct, how about you agree to go out with me, so you can learn about me?"

She thought he had been mad, but she said yes. The first thing he said was, "I know you shop at the personal beauty store around the corner."

She had stopped and looked at him with eyes widened by surprise. He held up his hands and took a step back.

"I can explain. I used to work in a large retail store where they sold makeup, and that color on your lips is amazing. I'm an architect, so I notice the details. It's not in the chain stores, I looked online, that limited it down to two stores. One of the stores is a tourist trap, so that left the other one around the corner."

Cora had been impressed with his thinking. She had been won over by his persistence, and she had eventually given her heart to him who cared more about her next breath than his own.

All that was still true if today was any indication, but too much had happened between them. A baby had happened between them. Coming to the camp would give her an opportunity to heal from her loss. Michael was right; she wasn't living. She was stuck. Cora knew the answer was to shed the past and start anew. That meant getting rid of Michael as well.

As she sat back in the chair and leaned her head on the headrest, she knew she would have had to be blind not to notice Michael. He was still an attractive man. With his snug shirt that lay on a muscled chest. His athleticly shaped body that narrowed to a vee at his waist, and his long and strong legs that leant their shape to the jeans he wore. He was still an attractive man that reminded her that she was still a living woman.

Michael never cared about his looks, but every woman who saw him would give him a second look one way or another. She let out a breath and tried to focus. She knew she should be able to withstand whatever Michael threw her way. Cora knew it was over for them, so this would just be a formality.

A small smile came to her lips. She wasn't sure what it was that Michael was planning, but she was sure it would be outrageous. Michael would be probably be surprised by the number of dates she had been on, trying to exorcise him from her memory.

No man had been able to take the place Michael held in her heart. No man had been able to make her smile like Michael. NO one had been able to take her mind away from her pain like Michael. The only problem was with the memory of Michael came the memory of Sophia. Her strong Sophia, who didn't get a chance to live.

Cora sniffed and shook her head. No, she wasn't going to go down that road. She knew what she was going to do. She was going to start over and stop living in the past. Right now, that meant showing Michael that there could be no them.

<h1 style="text-align:center">*Two*</h1>

Michael sat at his desk in the cabin. The early morning light shone into the room, allowing enough vision for Michael to see the bleak numbers on the screen. He didn't need the misty morning to remind him that all was not well in his personal life, or in his business life.

Normally, Michael wouldn't let the outside world affect him one way or another. However, he was a man who wouldn't turn away any encouragement. Even though Cora had said yes, it was tentative, and he knew he still had a massive climb in order to get her to believe in them again. That is, if it could be done.

"Are you sure you know what you're doing?" Veronica Green asked. "I have to meet with Cora in a little while. I told you I don't mind helping a person out, but it can't get in the way of the camp's purpose. The kids have to come first."

Michael looked over his shoulder at the rotund woman with black hair seated at her desk. Michael had known Veronica for the last four years they had partnered and participated in several charities for foster children and displaced families together. At the age of sixty-eight she was an imposing figure when she needed to be, and everyone's surrogate mother the rest of the time. Veronica was nicknamed Mama throughout the camp. Michael had never seen her in anything but blue jeans and blue-striped chambray tops.

During the last couple of years, Veronica had helped him to find ways to stay motivated, but most of all, she had helped him to keep Thalman Design after Cora had left.

"I don't know what I'm doing right now, Mama. I think I messed up in all kinds of ways. But still, when I left, she said she'd give me a chance."

"You know the chance might be superficial, right?" Veronica said with a shrug. "I know you want it bad, but sometimes things happen for a reason. Now, I haven't seen the girl, but I can tell you that losing a child is a hard hurdle to get over. Different women handle it in different ways, and then some never handle it at all."

Michael looked solemnly at her and thought of Cora. He thought of Cora smiling. He thought of Cora teasing him when she knew something he didn't. He knew there were a lot of unknowns, but he needed Cora, and he believed that Cora needed him as well.

"I didn't tell her about the problem with Thalman," Michael said as he looked at Veronica, who was giving him a disapproving look. "I know, I know I was supposed to do the whole thing, but I thought it was already too much trying to get her to let me work on our relationship. I didn't think it was the right time."

"Well, you better address that one way or another. Nothing makes a woman feel worse than thinking someone is trying to use her."

Michael had gone over the conversation several times. In retrospect, he could see how it had all gotten away from him. He hadn't expected her to say no.

"Cora has a mind that's amazing. She's always been able to think smarter and quicker than me, and I love her for it. I never thought I'd be on the receiving end of it," he said. "Who kicks someone out without knowing where they will sleep for the night?"

"Are you sure you know the woman she is today?" Veronica asked softly. "Life changes people, Michael. Have you considered that Cora has changed so much that you may have to give her the divorce because she's not the woman you once knew?"

Michael turned towards her and smiled. "I know it seems like she's not open to what it is that I want to do right now, but I know her. She said yes, and Cora doesn't say yes unless she plans on honoring the commitment. So while she hasn't opened her arms up to me the way she used to, I can tell there is still some part of the Cora that I knew, and still love, in there."

Michael couldn't tell Veronica the rest. He couldn't say to Veronica that Cora still called to him as a man. That if she had changed that much, she wouldn't appeal to him at all. In fact, the attraction to her was even stronger now than it had been before. He didn't know if it was because they had been separated for so long, but whatever it was, Michael always went with his gut, and his gut was saying he could reach Cora. He just hoped he still had a company left when it was done.

"I guess I thought if you told her about the company that would get you some extra points so she would consider giving you a chance?"

Michael cleared his throat and looked away.

"Michael?"

Holding his hands up in a defensive position, he came clean. "It's true that I didn't see a good time to mention the company, but at the end of the day, I wanted her to give us another try because she wanted us to get back together."

"Ah, so the onion is unwrapped layer by layer," Mama murmured. "Can you think of anything else you might have said or not said that I should know about?"

"You make it sound so ominous. I was in the same room with her. I think I should get a little leeway here."

Veronica gave him a stern look. "So you were overcome being in the same room with her. Were you under this spell for long? I mean, was it so enthralling that you couldn't remember that you happen to have a failing company that needs its COO back?"

Michael put his head back in his hands. "Okay, I couldn't do it. I couldn't bring up business just as I was getting somewhere. It's true I want her help with the company, and I'll ask, but she should come back for us. We are what's amazing."

"Did you tell her that?"

"I think I did. I think that's why she gave me a chance."

Veronica sighed. "Well, we'll see how it all plays out. This is her first time here, so I'll meet with her and make sure she understands how things work."

"No matter what happens, Mama, thanks."

Veronica walked up to Michael and pushed a lock of hair away from his forehead. "You're a good guy. A little reckless and headstrong, but that comes with youth."

"Hey, you make it seem like I'm a teenager," Michael said with a grin. "I told you I had a plan, and no matter what anyone thought about it, she said yes."

"Get out of here already. You're getting full of yourself, and nothing has happened yet." Veronica pursed her lips and shook her head. "Youth!"

Michael stood up and hugged Veronica. "You're the best. No matter what the rest of them say about you."

With that, he walked out of the main cabin. Directly across the dirt lane was the cabin he had stayed in last year with his friend, Evan. Michael had been there long enough that his was close to the main cabin and the entrance. He walked into the cabin, which was a carbon copy of the others. The door led into a large living room, and after four steps into the living room on the left-hand side, was a large eat-in kitchen. If you continued to walk straight through the living room, it fed into a hallway that led to the back door of the cabin and a wrap-around porch. When you went down the hallway, there was a door on the left and a door on the right. Each door led to a large bedroom.

Michael walked into the living room and saw all of his drawing supplies on the coffee table in the living room. The coffee table was littered with half-drawn charcoals of Cora. Michael sighed at the mess just as the door on the left opened and out walked his friend Evan. Every year Evan showed up and helped around the camp, he was an all-around handyman and one of Michael's closest friends.

"So I see Romeo has returned, but with no Juliette. Did you even convince her to let you stay with her?" Evan asked, shaking his head. Then he smiled. "I told you, man, women are the world's mystery. Are you still going on with this crazy plan?"

"I am, and it didn't sound so crazy when we thought about it a couple of weeks ago."

Evan stood with a towel wrapped around his waist and pulled the smaller towel from around his neck and dried his head. "A couple of weeks ago, my friend needed to have some hope. I was hoping that commonsense would come and save us both. Who knew you'd be crazy enough to actually try it?"

"Well, Cora said yes. So I take that as a great sign."

"Man, you have got it so bad. Since when is a woman kicking us out on the street a good sign?" Evan turned back to the hallway when he stopped drying his hair.

"Hey, did Mama tell you what you're doing this cycle?"

Michael waited. "No, go ahead and tell me."

"You've got tree house duty with two foster kids. They're brother and sister, so maybe it'll be fun."

Michael groaned. "Do you remember the last fun activity you did with your sibling?"

Evan laughed. "I'm an only child. I'm sure you'll figure it out. I mean, you're an architect. Oh, do you remember Melinda and Oliver from last year?"

"Yeah, they were nice enough. I think Melinda was a little skittish because she came with her sister, I think it was?"

"That's right. Well, they're all coming, and they've been assigned to the crew as helpers," Evan said. "It will be the merry band of misfits as we watch you try to win your true love."

Michael grinned at Evan's antics. "There will be no trying here. I will win her fair hand, and then you'll be coming to me for advice."

"Wow, man, get some more rest, because only sleep deprivation could make you think I need any help with woman," Evan said as he disappeared into his room.

Just as Michael was about to gather his drawings, there was a knock on the door, followed by Evan yelling from the room.

"Hey Michael, Ben is coming by, he wanted to touch base with you."

Michael rolled his eyes and went to the door. Ben Copton was Mama's right hand. He had been there in the beginning, and Mama had hired him when he had nothing. Ben was an older man with short cut hair and a bit of a paunch. The camp was a gift from Mama's grandson. Money wasn't an issue for her grandson, and Mama went out on a limb when she hired Ben. When Michael opened the door, Ben walked in. He went straight to the living room and began to stack the photos. After looking at the stacks on the table, he gave himself a nod and then looked to Michael.

Ben sat down and leaned back in one of the two chairs in the living room, then gave Michael a smile.

"So did all go well with Veronica? Were you able to talk about the setup and the finances of the camp?"

Michael shook his head because this was a sore point that Mama wouldn't even discuss. Michael imagined Ben trying to have this conversation at the same time he tried to straighten everything around him. Michael could see it not going well on several fronts.

"It's not an issue for the camp. I know there have been several offers for the camp, but I know that Mama isn't interested in selling."

"Have you looked at the books? If it wasn't for her grandson, you all know this place would go under.

We've received so many good offers to relocate and make a profit. I'm telling her she should look at it."

"We barely talked about the finances, but yes, it all went well. No, she's not going to sell even though she knows a generous offer was made. I think she's giving everyone a raise."

Ben huffed and then looked at the papers he still held in his hand.

"Well, with that behind us, I see there is a special guest you have here this cycle."

"Yes, she's special."

Ben stood up and nodded at Michael. "It seems the camp has opened up to be the love connection, but when we talk about dollars and cents, we can go ahead and brush that aside," he murmured.

"Ben, we're all doing our service here. We haven't forgotten why we're here or what we do."

Ben looked shocked. "I'm sorry Michael, I didn't mean to offend. I was just a little put out by how easy it was to get a meeting with Veronica for your cause, and I've been waiting for weeks to talk about the offer that was made to us all."

Michael knew Mama's feeling on the matter but didn't want to interfere. He had already asked Mama if she wanted him to resolve it with Ben, and she said no, she'd get to it.

Ben sighed into the silence. "Well, I've left your schedule on the table and the file on the kids you'll be with." Ben walked to the door and opened it. "Well, looks like fortune is with everyone but me, it seems there's someone else going into the main cabin."

Michael looked around Ben and saw Cora going into Mama's cabin. He let the door close behind Ben, and then he waited. Across the road, the two most important women in his life were meeting, and it didn't bring him any solace to know they were more than likely talking about him.

Three

It took less than ten minutes for him to be summoned via text to the cabin. Michael couldn't decide if it was a good or bad portent. He made sure he had on his neutral smile as he walked into the cabin. He didn't want to seem eager or just come out and say, "Hey ladies, did you decide in your wisdom to come up with another agreement?" Instead, he was going to play it cool and see what they threw at him.

He was prepared for a lot of things, but he wasn't ready to see them facing one another. This didn't look like an orientation. Instead, it looked like a standoff. Michael was lost and didn't know which way to go.

Veronica was sitting at the desk he was just in. She had a slight smirk on her face, but her back was straight. She radiated the vibe of a woman in charge. Michael looked at Cora, and he almost lost his composure. She was standing near a window on the side of the room. The light filtered around her, and she looked like the angel he had fallen in love with. She had a willowy figure that spoke of a gym and an active life. Cora had her arms crossed, and she turned to look out into the distance. He knew she was aware that the door had opened. That she didn't turn meant she knew who was coming through it.

Cora stood stiffly and Michael was unclear what to do. He waited for a sign from either one of them.

"Michael, come in, as this definitely involves you." Veronica gestured for him to come in as her eyebrow raised in good humor. "I can see the similar temperaments between you two. Cora told me you two have already talked and you've come to some agreements but after we spoke."

Michael was nervous about the word concession, but he held on to the idea that Cora had already agreed to stay. As long as she was here, he could work on them. He knew a couple of spots he might be able to take her for a picnic or to sit under the moonlight when they were done with the kids' activities. Ideas rolled about in his head. The concession he would work around, she was here, that's what mattered.

Michael smiled and turned toward Cora. "Regardless of how it happened, I'm happy you're here."

Cora turned to him, her lips pursed tightly together. Every so often her jaw clenched, a sure sign of her anxiety.

"Don't get happy just yet. I have a condition of my own if I stay."

Michael kept his smile in place and focused on Cora. "What do you want, Cora?"

Veronica cleared her throat, and Michael turned toward her, confused but waiting.

"Michael, Cora says she'll stay, but at no time does she want to be alone with you. She'll help the kids and do the activities without a problem."

"Can't be alone with me?" Michael was beyond shocked. He turned to Cora and shrugged his shoulders in despair. "You don't want to be alone with me? You thought you needed to have that as a condition? How can you say you're going to—"

"I am being true to my word Michael," Cora said in a low voice. "When we're together, you have the ability to cast a spell over me where I think everything can be done, and it will all be all right."

"And? That's bad?" Michael whispered.

"It's not bad, but I need to come out of that la-la land and live in the real world."

Michael took a step back and tried to clear his head. "I'm listening, but I don't understand."

Cora smiled sadly. "You make me forget, but when I'm not with you, it all comes tumbling in on me. I can't do that, Michael."

Michael looked at Veronica, hoping she would say something that would make this all a bad joke. Instead, she got up and put a hand to his shoulder, and then patted him as she walked by.

"I have no control of this, Michael, and at the end of the day, you two have to agree to these terms, not me."

Michael looked at Cora, tense with her sweater on and waiting. She hadn't brought a purse. She hadn't taken off her sweater. When he looked at her again, he saw her intentions. She was just waiting for him to say no.

"Michael?" Cora asked.

Michael shook his head. He had almost blown it and any chance to get back with Cora. She must be terrified to try this move. He turned towards Cora.

"I'm going to give you what you want Cora," he said, watching her. Cora let out a breath and then turned to Veronica.

"I told you he would never—"

Michael interrupted her. "We won't be alone."

"Do you still intend to work on your other objectives?" she asked coolly.

Michael smiled. "This little obstacle you've put up is a temporary setback. It's true you plan better, but I take more risks, and for you, Cora, I'm willing to risk it all."

Michael didn't wait for an answer. Instead, he tipped his head towards Veronica and then left the room. He didn't have a moment to lose. He had plans to make if he wanted to get his life back.

That man is crazy, and his antics only make me love him more, thought Cora as she heard the door close behind Michael.

"You're putting him in a bind," Veronica said.

"Yes, I am."

"Why?" Veronica asked as she gave Cora an intense look. "If you don't want him, just say so."

Cora looked out the window. "The question isn't about what I want."

Veronica looked at Cora for a moment longer and then chuckled. "You kids. If there was a long, difficult way to do something, you'd do it that way every time."

Cora shook her head. "You don't understand I—"

"You're right, I won't understand your pain. I had two miscarriages before I had my son. It's not your pain but pain nonetheless. What I can tell you is that there is pain in all of our lives. The only thing that makes it worth going on is finding someone to love through it all. Consider that as you are putting up all of these walls for Michael. Michael is a lot of great things, and he could use help in a lot of areas in his life, but if you're not seriously considering getting back with him, just leave tonight. He doesn't deserve to be hurt."

Cora looked at Veronica. "Why did you invite me if you didn't want me here?"

"Michael wanted you here, and Michael is like a son to me. If your question is, am I giving you the option to leave to protect Michael? Yes, I am. You kids today are a little too self-absorbed for me. I don't want Micheal to go through the pain of trying to win a person who isn't sure they want to be won or not. Love is hard. Everyone has to be onboard to make it work."

"I can't give you any guarantees. I can tell you that I'll—"

Veronica held up her hand. "I don't need promises now. If you come up to a decision that it's not going to be, we'll deal then. For now, we need to make sure you understand that no matter what is going on, this camp is about the kids."

Cora nodded in agreement. "So, what else does he need?"

Veronica stopped and eyed her closely. "Need?"

Cora smiled. "I know, Michael and it's simple so what else does Michael need."

Veronica gave her a smile. "I like you, Cora. I've interfered enough. The rest of this, you two will have to work out. At any rate, I want you to know that I'm grateful that you're here. We struggle to find people who want to volunteer time at the camp."

Cora laughed. "I think this is a wait-and-see moment, but I want to thank you for having me."

Veronica nodded. "I have the benefit of age. Out with you."

Cora nodded, then walked out of the cabin and made it back to hers. She had a lot to think about, but more importantly. She had to prepare for Michael.

Four

Cora was on the road to go back to her cabin when she noticed the larger cabins across the way. Looking up the path, she didn't see Michael, so she assumed he must have gone into one of them. The first cabin she ran into read 'Meeting Center.' She was never to let something just sit. She decided that the way Michael left wasn't good for either of them.

The building was cool, and the reception desk was empty. When she heard Michael's voice, she followed it until she found him. She went to a nearby open door and walked in. Michael was next to an older man with a table between them while the older gentleman pointed to papers on the table. She cleared her throat, and both of them looked up.

Michael's head popped up and he looked relieved. While the other gentleman narrowed his gaze and approached her.

"You must be Cora? Welcome to Second Chance Camp. I'm Ben Copton. If the title is to be believed, I'm the Assistant Manager at this camp."

Cora took his hand in a brief shake. His hands were cold and clammy. She hadn't wanted to shake his hand,

and when they touched, she couldn't wait to get her hand back. His initial glower at her put her on alert. When she saw that Michael was relieved, a part of her wanted to stand up and ask Michael what was wrong.

"Well, Mr. Copton, I'll probably be coming to see you often, with me being the newbie here."

"I'm around if you need anything," Michael offered.

Cora nodded and gave Michael a small smile. "I know, but I like to know who to go to when things go awry or when I need an explanation on things. Like Mr. Copton said, he works here. Is that correct, Mr. Copton?"

Ben's smile froze in place, and he gave a small nod. "Of course. I'm here for the camp."

"That's good to hear. I'm sorry I interrupted you two. I'll meet up with Michael later."

Michael nodded and then held up his hand. "I wanted to bring some papers for you to look at, so we'll be over later."

Cora stilled and gave him a look. "Papers? You do remember the conditions?"

"Oh yes, I do. So my friend, Evan and I will be by in the morning, to give you time to settle in," Michael said as he walked out of the door. Mr. Copton nodded his head and walked out behind Michael.

She didn't know what Michael was up to, but she had a feeling she better rest up today so she pulled herself together and continued to her cabin.

"What do you mean I have to go with you to Cora's cabin?" Evan said as he sat across from Michael at the breakfast nook the next morning. Michael had waited until Evan had food before he explained to his friend about Cora's stipulation.

"Cora doesn't want to be alone with me. So I need someone to be with us. You're doing administrative work this cycle, so I'm asking you."

"Wow, looking at you, I'm hoping this love thing doesn't catch me. So I'm going to be the chaperone for you?" Evan asked, lifting his eyebrows humorously.

"Whatever, are you going to do it or not?"

Evan reached out for a biscuit that was on the table and nodded. "I want to go on the record as saying I'm doing this for you, and you will owe me majorly if you two get back together."

Michael shook his head. "I know, I know."

"Then yes, you've got yourself a chaperone for this cycle."

Michael let out a sigh of relief and then looked at his watch. "Well, get dressed, we need to go to her cabin."

Evan peeked at the window. "Now?"

"Yes, now? What else were you doing?"

Evan shrugged. "I was going to get some food—"

Michael looked at him incredulously. "How can you possibly stay fit with all the junk food you eat?"

"Because I earn heaven points by being a chaperone for my friends," he said.

Once they made it out of the door Evan asked, "So, why are we going over this morning?"

"I need Cora to look at some paperwork?"

Evan shook his head. "Dude, tell me you've told her that you need her help."

Michael let out a deep breath. "I wanted to, but she came up with this condition, and then I forgot."

Evan guffawed. "You forgot to tell your estranged wife, who you're trying to win over, that the company the two of you built together is in financial trouble and you need her to save you? One of those, maybe, but all of them, Mike?"

"I know it sounds bad."

"I don't get it. You are one of the most sought after men in the city. I've seen you spec out a building in a heartbeat, and everyone is amazed."

"Yeah, well, I can see a picture no problem, but these contracts have more pitfalls in them than a few. Have you read some of them? I think they put in old English and so many subsections that it tires you out. Then the last section always seems to imply you should ignore all other sections and give it all up."

Evan laughed. "So let's ask the important questions. Do you think Cora can, and is willing, to help you?"

Michael smiled. "There's nothing she can't do. Cora always handled contracts because she can't Design to save her life, but if it's written on paper, that woman can read it in three seconds and write a reply that will make them all think it was their idea."

Evan smiled. "If you know she has the answer, why are we walking like old women to her cabin?"

Michael gave Evan a frustrated face, picked up his pace, and gripped the papers in his hands a little tighter. "I want more from her than to just fix our company. I want my wife back."

"Well, the word is you can charm a snake."

"I'm hoping I can live up to that reputation." When they arrived at the cabin, Michael squared his shoulders and knocked on the door. Moments later, Cora appeared in front of him.

Cora was dressed in business casual. She had on black slacks and a beige top. She was lean, professional, and as attractive as ever. So it seemed like she wasn't going to make this easy at all. She looked amazing.

She gave him a small smile.

"Good morning Michael. It's early, try to focus," she said as she stepped back to let them in.

When she closed the door, she led them to the kitchen nook where she had some biscuits in a basket on the table.

"Gentlemen, would you like some coffee?"

"I'm still in awe, I made it in twice by invitation."

Cora gave him a bland smile. "There's still time to remedy that mistake."

Evan cleared his throat. "Excuse me." Evan looked between them both and then grabbed a biscuit. "Listen up, I understand that for whatever reason, I'm playing chaperone, but if there's going to be verbal battling, I'm going to need more food than this."

"More food than that? There's no way you can finish all of those, and we're not having a verbal anything."

Evan reached for another biscuit. "Okay, I'm just throwing that out there."

Cora sat across from Michael, "Why are we having this meeting, Michael?"

Michael put the papers on the table and slid them across to Cora.

She picked them up and read over a couple of pages. Her face never changed, and Michael didn't know what to expect. When she put the papers down, she folded her arms over her chest and raised an eyebrow.

"Michael, you really need to have someone look these over before you sign them."

"I do have someone, but she took a sabbatical, and I thought I could do it until she came back," he replied.

Cora froze in place. "You should have updated your thinking when I didn't come back within the month. These contracts are almost ironclad."

Michael looked at Cora and knew the time had would come.

"Cora, I need you to save our business."

"You could find have found so many competent people to address."

Michael could feel Evan's eyes on him, and for a moment, he thought about not saying anything and letting it go. Then he straightened his back and laid it out on the line.

"If I can't get past the ridiculous demands in those contracts, she is going to wind up owning parts of Thalman's Design. I have to tell you, I'll close the doors first."

Cora took a deep breath and gave him an assessing look.

"You love that company," she whispered.

Michael smiled. "Then help me save it, please."

Cora was taken aback. He could tell by the stunned look on her face. Then she looked over at Evan and then back at him. "Okay, as long as it doesn't interfere with my camp duties."

Michael smiled. "Speaking of that, can you look at a contract that's been sent to the camp. An investor wants the camp to move to another spot and says they can offer us a comparable deal."

Cora reached for a muffin, only to discover the basket was empty. She looked at Evan, who tried to look innocent, but it was hard to do so with an incriminating crumb on his chin.

"You ate them all," Cora said.

Evan shrugged. "I think you were answering the question. Then we can go get some more biscuits." Evan said optimistically.

Michael cleared his throat. "Cora?"

Cora looked at Michael and nodded. "Anyone else read the developer contract?"

"Just Ben."

"No worries, I'll do it. But if that contract looks like the one you signed earlier, I'd be surprised if you haven't already given her a date to take everything, and you just didn't know it."

"We're not that gullible."

Cora looked at him skeptically.

"Okay, what I should say is that Veronica hasn't signed it because it hasn't been a priority for her, and she doesn't need the money. I think she's decided not to, but she wants to be sure she makes an informed decision."

Cora nodded.

Evan clapped, and Michael and Cora jumped. "Well, I'm glad that's done. It's time for me to go. The food is gone, and this chaperone thing is making me hungry. So I'll see you later, Cora."

Evan waved at Cora and headed toward the door. Michael stood up.

Michael looked at Evan's retreating back. "Since we'll be meeting up a bit, you might want to reconsider this condition, or get a lot more food for Evan." He bent his head and placed a light kiss on her forehead.

She paused but didn't pull away, and again, he held on to every positive sign he could get from her. As long as he had a chance, he'd keep going.

Five

Later, outside of her cabin, Cora sat on her mat. She had taken up evening meditation to calm herself. When she meditated, it allowed her to focus on nothing and bring calm to her being. That calmness helped her to think and function.

Michael had brought several contracts to her door, and he hadn't come alone. In fact, each time he came he brought one of the other counselors to meet her. She had gone through the documents and could see Thalman's Design needed some help. There was something that wasn't quite right about the contracts.

She was tired when evening came, and meditating gave her time to review the day. Michael, that man, could still pull the strings on her heart. When he came to the door, he was polite and sweet, just like he was when she first met him. He made sure whoever was with him introduced themselves, and he let them lead when it came to talking about themselves. That was Michael. He was the one who would always let her shine. He was egoless, and so compassionate that in the end, that compassion had been her problem.

He never once blamed her when they lost Hope.

She tried to clear her head. Cora tried to find that place where there was nothing but calmness, and now the only thing she could see was Michael. Micheal with open arms. Michael laughing when he had done something silly. Michael crying with her as they lay in their bed.

These were the days when it was too much. These were the days when she finished meditating and found tears streaming down her face. She opened her eyes and realized that her breath was rapid, but her face was dry. It was then that she opened her eyes, looked down in her lap and realized that she had thought about Hope and didn't have tear stains on her yoga pants.

She touched the grey pants and took a deep breath. Cora wanted to indulge in the moment, but a shadow was cast over her, and the moment was gone.

"Hello, I'm Melinda Tavers, the camp organizer," a woman's voice said.

Cora looked up and saw a familiar woman standing with a man by her side and two children. She recognized the woman from around the camp.

"This gentleman is Howard and these two darlings behind us are Lily and Peter Stevens. We wanted to come by and introduce ourselves. Lili and Peter have been assigned to you and Michael this cycle."

This woman is way too chipper, Cora thought as she tried not look at her too skeptically. Cora had seen Melinda around the camp yesterday as she was processing. Everywhere she went people smiled and acquiesced to Melinda. It wasn't her height, because Melinda was five foot even, at most. She had dark hair and a waif-like body. Cora supposed she was fashionably thin. Today Melinda was dressed in jeans and a camp tee shirt.

If she hadn't introduced herself, she might have mistaken her for one of the kids.

"Hello, everyone," Cora said, giving them all a nod and a smile. "I thought we were going to meet tomorrow at breakfast, but it's good to meet you."

"All of this meeting could wait, in my opinion," Howard said morosely. Cora had to suppress her smile when she looked at Howard. He was maybe five foot eleven and thin. He screamed unemployed artist. His jeans were stained with paint, he wore a checkerboard shirt, and he was lanky, with only lean muscle mass that Cora guessed was what he needed to lift his artwork.

The overall effect was a talented grunge. With a mass of black hair that looked like it had only every known a finger comb and blue eyes that were so bright they looked translucent.

Howard was the definition of a bohemian artist, and she could see how he would fit on the camp to inspire foster kids.

"I have several works that are drying, and I've already started my charges on their work, so while I was drafted to welcome you here, I'm hoping this isn't a long term event."

Cora listened to him, and she was sure a sloth would sound just like him, if it could talk. Howard's voice was slow, and he enunciated every word. The only time she saw any life in him was when he said the word art. Howard cleared his throat and nodded.

"You don't look like you're into art. Gina was into art," Howard added. "You are here to take Gina's place, right?"

"That is what's supposed to happen," Cora replied. She was about to get up when she saw the boy who must have been Peter. He was skinny with a frame that suggested one day he'd be a great football candidate. He had a tan most women would kill for and black hair that was bone straight. His jeans were ripped, but it was unclear if they were like that due to the current style or because of his circumstances. His jaw was tight and Cora guessed he was about fourteen years old at best, but he clearly had a chip on his shoulder that said he was ready to take on the world. Maybe it was the way his eyes darted to and fro as if they were waiting for something to happen. He didn't smile, and he didn't say hello. He just nodded his head in greeting.

Cora stood up, feeling uncomfortable meeting them from the floor. She felt as though she had to make sure the kids saw her as the authority figure and not some last minute push over.

"I can see this is going to be all that I thought it would be," Cora said.

"Then I'm not the only one who thought this wasn't going to work," the girl, who Melinda had called Lili, muttered. "We come to get a break from the foster life, and the first thing we find out is we're being passed off to someone else. This doesn't feel like a break at all," she said. She was seventeen going on ninety. She looked like the older one of the two, but what the age difference was she couldn't tell. What was obvious was the relation between the two. She was a more delicate version of the boy. Her body was lithe and had the hint of curves that heralded a beauty in the making.

Lili was wearing a camp tee shirt and black jeans. Her hair was pulled back into a ponytail. With her hair up, it emphasized her long neck and fine bone structure. Lili was attractive now and as she got older her beauty would definitely turn more heads.

Lili stood with her arms crossed over her chest. "I guess you didn't have a choice about being at the camp either. So this is going to be a great time since none of us wanted to be here," Lili said gruffly.

"I have to tell you I didn't get to choose who'd I'd be with during this camping experience but I'll make sure all is taken care of to the best of my ability," Cora said as she brushed off her yoga pants.

"It seems we are all going to be altering plans. I was just given a new schedule," Melinda stated. "I've been doing the schedule for the camp since almost the beginning, but now it has to be reviewed."

Cora noticed the tension in Melinda's voice. "Maybe it's just a part of the investors looking," Cora said, trying to soothe the situation. Two sets of eyes looked on with interested.

"Maybe, but that's another conversation I wasn't really in either."

"Perhaps we can talk about it at another time," Cora said. "We have the kids here now."

Peter laughed. "Don't worry, we are used to having adults argue in front of us. Adults do that really well."

Cora looked at Peter and sighed. Not only did he come across as having a chip, but he had also come from some hard times as well from the sound of it. She turned toward Melinda and Howard. "I want to thank you for coming, but I need to take a shower and get some dinner."

Melinda nodded. "Well, that was in the plan as well. The changed plan. All of the counselors are meeting for dinner tonight at the main cabin across from where you met with Veronica. Everyone is expected."

Cora put on a smile. "Well, then I'll be seeing you soon?"

Howard shook his head. "Not the kids. They've been spared and can do whatever they want. It'll be us and the other counselors."

Cora didn't even know what to say to Howard. At an event dedicated to the kids she expected them to be able to attend avery event.

"Well, like I said, I've got to get ready for the event."

"Well, we'll see you at dinner then," Melinda said.

Cora turned and went into her cabin. She never thought that she'd be happy to escape two kids and two adults, but this camp was turning out to be a little more than she thought. First Michael, then the contracts and now the odd conditions she saw in the contracts. This would be the last time that she did a friend a favor.

Six

An hour later there was a knock on her cabin door, and Cora dreaded opening it. She had just gotten her shower done and clothes on. She didn't have an excuse to stay in the cabin. It was time to face the music.

"Coming," she said, expecting to see Melinda on the other side. She opened the door, and there stood Michael with his cell phone next to his face and Evan on the screen waving back.

"I wanted to make sure I kept to the rules, so I have Evan on FaceTime. He's with us, so we're not alone. Say hi, Evan."

"Hi, Cora!" Evan said as he took a bite out of something. "I'm at the main cabin, and the snacks are warm and plentiful."

Cora looked at the phone and then at Michael and groaned to stop the laughter that was bubbling up. Micheal was dressed in black jeans and a blue shirt that outlined a well-defined chest. His hair was still wet, and he had that smile on his face that made her forget her thoughts.

"Cora, in case I didn't say it. You like nice."

"Hey, I'm on the phone here. She looks nice, grab her hand and bring her to the cabin," Evan called out.

Michael held out his other hand. "Come on, Cora. I'm playing by your rules. Let's go eat."

"Sure you are," Cora said with a grin. "I could have walked over by myself, you know. It would have been relaxing after my shower."

"I know you could find your way, but I was looking for an excuse to see you."

Cora looked at him suspiciously. "We'll be working together with our charges, who I've had the pleasure of meeting."

"I can see it in your eyes how moved you were. Let's get going before Evan eats everything."

"I heard that," Evan said.

Cora watched Michael mute the phone but leave the face time on. As they walked down the path, Cora was nervous, expecting Michael would begin talking about them. Instead, he did what he always did, the unexpected.

"So have you read the contracts and found out if I've given away the farm?"

Cora was relieved that he hadn't started in on the past. "I'm surprised that you asked me that. If you knew you were doing that, why did you sign the contract?"

"I needed to get the work done, and I figured since the contract was so short, how bad could it be?"

"It could be horrible. I'll write up the notes, but let's just say you need to make sure you get all of your deadlines."

"You know she has to approve work she's involved in before she releases her permits."

Cora nodded. "My gut tells me this didn't just happen like this accidentally."

Michael ran his hand through his hair. "I went out to lunch with her a couple of times, and when she offered to help, I thought it was great."

"And…"

"And all the time I thought she was just a friend and…"

Cora prodded him along. "And then what?"

"And then I told her about this plan I had to get you back, and she became a whole different woman."

Cora shook her head and laughed. "Really, Michael?"

Holding up his hands. "I was transparent. I told Glory in the beginning, you are my world. I told her you are amazing at everything you set your mind to. And then it just went south. Then she offered to handle some paperwork, one friend helping another and the next time I knew it we were doing business together but it didn't seem bad so I didn't fight it. I just didn't want to be bothered with anything that reminded me of what I had lost."

"Well, thank you for the compliment. I don't know that I do all those things, but it's good to know what you think of me."

Michael cleared his throat. "You know me, Cora. What I said isn't for show. You are the woman I still dream about," he said in low tones. "Even after everything we've been through. I don't know a woman who could compare. I know we need to talk about Hope."

"Please—"

"It'll come when you're ready, but no matter what, I want you to know it's always going to be about us. I'll be here for you when you're ready."

Cora stopped walking. They were a few feet from the cabin.

"What if I'm never ready, Michael. You can't hold your life up. Thalman Designs needs a contractor to help you. You need to find out how to replace me in your life."

Michael shook his head and took a step back.

"You don't get it Cora. There's no life without you. A piece of me is missing, and I need it to see the beauty in the world. Right now, what you see is me on borrowed time."

"And if I can't remember who we were?" Cora asked through clenched teeth.

Michael held out his hands and walked up to the cabin. "I don't know, Cora. I can't even imagine it."

Walking into the room was a different experience than it had been yesterday with Ben and Michael. The inhabitants of the room were broken up into small cliques. It felt like high school all over again. Evan had greeted Michael by the door, but as they moved into the room, Evan left for the food tables off to the side. Michael moved to the side and stood by the window with a cola can in his hand.

She saw people walk by him, give him dirty looks and then continue on as if he were a party crasher. Cora didn't see anyone going to stand with him, and her anger at everyone in the room started to rise. She walked over to Michael just as Howard and Melinda rounded on him.

"It seems like you should be taking care of the contracts instead of being here," Howard said mournfully.

Micheal lifted his can. "As well as I read contracts, I might do more good here."

"Well, I used to take care of things, but since you came, things are changing, and since I'm being left out, I can't really help, can I?" Melinda said.

"Things change all the time. At the end of the day, this will be whatever Veronica wants."

The two moved on, and as Cora stood apart from him, she saw a member or two of the staff shake their heads. Finally, Cora couldn't take it anymore, and she walked up when a couple was standing in front of Michael, grilling him as if he were a thief.

"We've all been here with Veronica," the woman said. "How can it be that you get taken into her confidence with our fates."

"If you don't like it, you can always go to Veronica and speak to her yourself," Michael said as he chugged the last of his soda.

The man snorted and narrowed his eyes. "We used to discuss everything as a group. Now that you've come it's whatever you decide you want to do this year. Why don't you just admit that you've already sold this place to one of your fancy architect people?"

Cora cleared her throat, and the couple jumped.

"It never ceases to amaze me how people who know nothing of the details of a situation feel the need to give their uninformed opinion," she said curtly. "Fortunately for you all, Michael has asked someone who understands contracts to assist."

The couple turned en masse on her, and Cora stood her ground, waiting.

"If the rumors are true, the only reason Michael is still here—and for that matter the only reason Second chance camp is still here—is because of you. Everyone knows that the camp had some money problems and you and your grandson helped us when no one else would," the woman said. "So, I guess when you're tired of this, we'll lose this place."

Cora tried to control her breathing and realized that the level of fear running through the camp was making them all crazy. Crazy or not, she wasn't going to let them beat up on Michael.

"I'm here because a friend asked me to take her place. Everything else that may or may not be happening with Michael and me is secondary. I came here to help, just like everyone else did."

Melinda walked over to the group and stood with her arms crossed over her chest. "You weren't here before, and now we all know he's letting you read the contracts. For someone who just showed up, you seem to be the one in charge. What exactly are your intentions here to—?"

Michael cut off Melinda. "This conversation is over."

Howard frowned. "We were just—"

Michael took a step away from the wall. "Listen to me, all of you. Cora will not directly or indirectly take the brunt of your misplaced fears. A friend asked her to come, and she did. I asked her for help, and she agreed. Neither one of those requests has to do with any of you, and you are not included in them. Cora is off-limits, is that clear?"

The couple nodded, and Melinda and Howard walked away rattled. She looked at the retreating crowd and let out a sigh. Normally, she was the one fending off the crowds. She made sure her employees were treated right. She advocated for them and made sure her work ethic was exemplified in every project. One of the many things that she had missed about Michael was the way he would stand and defend her against anyone or thing. It was tenuous and light, but she felt that familiar bond between them starting to form.

There was nothing but silence between them as everyone else had moved away. She turned to find him standing there, waiting for her to acknowledge him.

"Are you okay?" he asked in a low voice.

That voice. Cora looked at Michael and then closed her eyes and hung her head. This man was the defender in one breath and the compassionate comforter the next.

"Thanks."

"Always."

"You know I thought if we were surrounded by people that I would be able to keep you at a distance," she confessed.

He gave a sad smile. "I know."

"I was wrong," she whispered. She gave him a smile and then took his hand. "You want to go on a walk?"

"You didn't eat."

She gave him a smile. "I'm not hungry."

Michael nodded. "Let me get Evan—"

Cora reached out and stopped him. "I think we can do this one on our own."

"All right."

Seven

Michael didn't question his good fortune, he followed Cora out of the cabin and onto the path. They walked in silence for a while, and when they reached her cabin, he pointed out a small playground that was behind her circle.

They found a bench, and he waited as long as he could.

"Sorry about tonight. As usual, I think you handled it like a pro," Michael said.

"Thanks. I've learned how to take care of myself and my employees."

The weather was just warm enough for them to sit on the bench. He thought about taking her back to her place, but he wasn't ready to give up the moment.

"Are you cold?"

"No, I'm good. Oh goodness, this is so awkward, Michael."

He wanted to reach out to her and make it better. He wanted to erase the time that had passed between them, and although he had planned for this moment, he wasn't sure what he should do now. So he smiled and did what he knew. He went with his gut.

"It's me, Cora. How can this be awkward?"

He heard her take in a deep breath. "Nothing is the same anymore. It hasn't been the same since Hope."

It was the first time he'd heard her say their daughter's name, and he wanted to turn to her and pull her into his embrace to let her know she wasn't alone, but he was scared that it would break the moment.

"I can hear you thinking so hard, Michael."

"I'm letting you lead here, Cora."

He saw her wringing her hands in her lap, and still, he waited.

"Well, the long and short of it is, we lost a daughter. I was hurt, and I pushed you away so we wouldn't talk about it…" He looked at her and saw her blinking back pain-filled tears.

"You needed time," he said as he reached his hand out to cover hers.

She sniffed and gave him a wan smile. "No, the truth of it was I wasn't strong enough. I had failed you both and—"

"Don't Cora. You weren't alone, and we both made mistakes."

She reached over and ran her pointer finger along his chin. "Let me finish this."

Michael was confused, and it must have shown because she moved her finger from his chin to his lips. He closed his eyes and kissed her fingertips. Time fell away.

The last time he had kissed her fingertips, they had been at a park, and he had held her in his arms. It was Thalman's employee party. He had chased her behind a large oak tree. She had placed her fingertips over his lips when one of the project managers had called out his name.

Cora had smiled at him and leaned down and placed her lips over his. Before her lips had touched him she whispered the secret that she had been holding to her heart all day long.

"We're going to have a baby," she whispered. Then she had kissed him, with joy on her lips and love in her eyes. The kiss hadn't lasted long. It was just enough to get him to want more. Then like a schoolgirl without a care in the world, she had spun out of his embrace and run back toward the company picnic area.

Her eyes had been warm and inviting. There had been a glow to her cheeks and a beauty that comes with pregnancy.

Today that joy was gone. Her fingertips trembled against his lips, and she looked at him with such a forlorn expression, he wanted to tell her that whatever it was didn't matter.

"I want to tell you something, Michael. When I do, maybe I can get past the rest, but I know as long as I don't..." she broke off, her breath ragged breath.

He stared at her and waited. Whatever it was, he'd stand with her.

"After Hope, I went to the doctor and found that the genetic issue that led to her death was in me."

He heard the pain in her voice and reached out to lift her head so they would be looking in each other's eyes.

"Don't do this, Cora. Sometimes things happen—"

"This isn't a sometimes thing. All the other times when it didn't happen. It was me. I knew something then Michael. I would never take the chance of bringing a child into the world. I went to a doctor, and I got a hysterectomy."

"Alone?"

He saw the tears course down her face. "I did it alone."

"Did you think I'd love you less?"

"Afterward, I knew we couldn't get back together. You always wanted a family. I couldn't do that and—"

"Who went with you to the hospital?"

Cora pulled back and wiped her face. "No one."

Micheal stared at her for a moment before he frowned. "I could have lost you both, and I would have never known why."

"Michael—"

"I can't say I understand because I don't. I thought we were a team no matter what? I thought—"

Cora jumped to her feet. "I was wrong, Michael, to go alone. I don't regret what was done or what I did. I stand by it. But I was wrong not to include you. I was just in so much pain, and you were so perfect. The doctor had already told me I was the problem and you were talking about trying again and…"

Micheal stood and looked at Cora, defiant and proud. She was tough. She had endured so much already, and still, she found the strength to tell him. It was so much to take in at once, and he wasn't sure what to think or feel.

Cora took a step closer to him and then kissed him on the cheek.

"I told you this so you'd know who I am now. I told you because you had a plan, but I may not be the woman you thought you were getting. Get some rest and think about it. There's still time for us to petition to

Melinda and get new assignments if necessary. You know where to find me."

Michael sat down on the bench and waited until Cora had disappeared around the bend. Then he put his head in his hands and cried.

Eight

It was the last day before she would meet the kids. She had to go to the seminars on a day in the life of a foster care child. She learned how to know when it was time to let a counselor know about issues. All of the information was new to Cora and gave her new insights into the children. She was engaged, but at the end of the day, when she was alone, the conversation she had with Michael came back to her.

Just when she was about to change her clothes, she heard a knock at her door. When she opened it, Michael was standing on the porch. She had just left him in the cabin during orientation, but he was on the other side of the room. Cora hadn't made a move toward him, still unsure of how he felt.

"Michael?"

His mouth twitched. "Yes, I've been me all day long," he said.

"Don't be a smart aleck," she said, standing in the door.

"I wasn't sure if you'd let me in," he said.

She sighed. "I think we can put that rule away."

"Can I come inside?" he asked.

Cora stepped aside and showed him in. Her stomach began to roll with dread as she took a seat on her couch. Michael was either going to tell her he forgave her or she was as wrong as she had been calling herself all of these years. This was her nightmare and her dream all rolled up in one. She led him into her living room, and they sat down.

"Cora, it's me," he said.

She sighed and tried not to fidget. This was Michael. At the end of the day, this was an overdue conversation no matter what happened. The silence stretched on.

"Michael?"

"I thought about it, and I wanted you to know, I'm sorry you went through it alone. Even after everything you said, I know there's still an us. I know we love each other Cora, but I don't think we know each other anymore the way we should."

"Okay," she said uncertainly. Confused, she sat back on the couch and shrugged her shoulders. "What does that mean, Michael?"

"It means I want us to get to know each other again. What I'm saying is, I'd like to date you again."

She sat back, but still, the confusion ran amuck in her head.

"So we're…starting over?"

He reached out and covered her hand. "Not starting over from scratch. Have no doubt Cora, I love you. I think right now, we just don't know each other like we should."

"So, how do we do this?"

Michael grinned and looked at Cora. "We can start tonight."

"Tonight?"

"Yes, we can start tonight if you don't mind staying in."

Cora laughed. "Then, this is a lot like when we first started dating."

"Come on, Cora, we've gone out to some nice places."

"We have, but in case you don't remember, the first place you took me—when you paid—was a hot dog stand."

"Okay, you got me," he laughed. "Okay, this is what I'll do. Next date, I'll take you on a real date."

"With flowers and a restaurant?"

Michael nodded solemnly. "I guess I can find a restaurant with flowers."

"I'm so grateful," Cora chuckled as she listened to Michael and eventually fell back on the couch in a fit of laughter. It felt so good to finally be able to laugh about something. The laughter washed away the gloom "Okay, so what are we doing on this first date?"

Michael smiled and then reached over and put her hands on hers.

"First, I tell you what you already know. I like you, Cora."

"Really? Well, I think you like everyone so big deal," she replied in a slow voice, looking at their hands. How long had it been since she had seen her hands in Michael's man's? Michael's hands were warm and steady. There was no indecision or clamminess in them.

"I do like everyone to a certain degree, but you are special. I like the others because I can leave them when I feel like it. I like you, because I don't want to leave you, ever."

"Ever?" she whispered.

"Yes, love, this is for the long game."

Cora looked up into his eyes, and she felt the moment of stepping into the abyss. Her hands tightened up, and she looked away from him. His hand went to her chin and then lifted it up.

"Cora, breathe with me." His other hand went back and forth over hers.

She wanted to tell him that she didn't need him to tell her to breathe. She wanted to tell him that the only time she needed to remember to breathe was when she was nervous or fearful. She wasn't either of those things now—at least that's what she wanted to be able to say. Unfortunately, her increasing heartbeat and short breath as signaling something contrary to that.

"Cora Thalman," he said, smiling into her eyes. "I don't want you to think I'm too forward, but I'd really like to kiss you."

It was as if she were in a faraway land. She knew it was Michael. She knew so much tragedy was between them, but right now, right now listening to him, she had to admit she was willing to grab on to the lifeline of hope his words spun for her. She nodded her head.

She thought he would just pull her into his arms and kiss her senseless. That it would be a big whirlwind movie-worthy type of pull into his arms. Instead, he picked up her hand and intertwined their fingers. She looked at their hands twined together and then back at him.

"I'm not going to jump you, Cora. I think I have a little more self-control than that. This time it will be all about you and doing things on your time."

"You may never kiss me if I have to wait on you to get there."

He laughed. "It just means when I get there, we'll both definitely be ready."

She waited for him to say he was joking or in some way take over but he didn't. The ball of tension that had wound itself into a hardcore began to loosen itself. "Michael, I need you to help me."

He inched closer to her and brought their hands up between them. He smiled, leaned in and then pressed his lips to hers. It was barely a kiss by anyone's standards, much less Michael's. The confusion must have shown on her face. Michael lifted their joined hands higher.

"We both need this barrier between us tonight. This won't be the whirlwind, Cora."

She looked down to see his hands trembling ever so slightly. Those trembles were enough to make her relax and for once believe that she and Michael were in equally vulnerable positions. She let out a breath and gave him a tentative smile.

"No, I guess it won't be a whirlwind."

He leaned in and she was sure he was going to kiss her, but instead, he let his forehead rest against hers. She couldn't explain it but it was the last thing she expected, and she realized it was the thing she needed the most. It was nurturing and touching all at the same time.

"It's time for me to go," he said as he let her hand go and then went to the door.

She followed him and cleared her throat. "O-Okay," she said hesitantly, beating herself up mentally for stammering like some school girl.

He turned when he got to the door, and she had to stop herself abruptly to not run into him.

"Cora."

"Yes?"

"Dream of me and remember us," he said as he pressed a chaste kiss to her forehead and stepped out the door. She closed the door behind him and then leaned against it.

Remember us. Cora thought she wasn't going to be able to do anything else but remember them.

Nine

The knock on the door brought a smile to Cora's face. She pulled it open expecting to see Michael. He was an hour early, and she was already thinking of the meager fixings she could put together to feed him and talk.

But it was the teen Peter on her doorstep. He was dressed in a camp tee shirt and black jeans. Every so often, he looked over his shoulder and then at the door.

"Hello, Peter. It's good to see you."

"I guess." He appeared to be looking around Cora to see if there was anyone else behind her. "Mind if we talk?"

Cora gave him a long look. She could tell he thought she was going to say yes right away and had already started to walk toward the entrance. When he realized that she hadn't moved, he stopped looking over his should and then gave her his full attention.

"Do you have a problem talking out here?"

His eyebrows went up in surprise for a moment and then he nodded.

"Are we speaking truth?" he asked.

Cora nodded. "That is the only thing I expect to speak between us."

"I want to talk and I'm not supposed to be here. I don't want to get caught out here, so I'd prefer to talk inside."

Cora stepped back and allowed him to come into her cabin.

"Thanks."

"Do you want something to drink? Water or chocolate?"

Peter stepped in and looked around before going toward the kitchen. He laughed and took a seat at her table.

"For a minute there, I thought you were going to offer me some milk and cookies."

Cora followed him into the kitchen and prepared some coffee for them both.

"I admit my entertaining skills with teens is rusty at best," Cora confessed.

"And you're here volunteering at a foster camp?" Peter asked.

Cora nodded. "It's complicated."

"That's what adults say when they've been caught doing something wrong, or they have no idea what the answer is."

"That's enough, smarty, what did you want to talk to me about?" Cora asked as she took a seat across from Peter. The boy had sass and vinegar, as her elderly aunts would say.

"The rumor is you're here because your man is trying to get you back. The way I see it, I can help you out if you're willing to help me out," Peter said. His countenance had changed from easygoing, to all business. It was heartbreaking to see that type of fierce determination etched into such a young face. She was so taken aback by the grimness in his gaze that she didn't even comment on the fact that he knew about Michael's plan.

"What is it that you think I can do for you?"

Peter sat back in his chair and tried to look relaxed and in control. If the situation wasn't so serious, she'd think it was funny the way he was trying to control the meeting with his body language. One day, Peter Stevens would be a formidable man. Today, she had to wrangle with the boy-man.

"We need to agree before I say what I want," Peter said.

"I'm not sure I can agree to anything. If I can, I'll help you out, but it all depends on what you would like me to do. I won't do anything wrong or illegal. So tell me what you would like me to do?"

"I want you to hear me first, and then I'll let you think about it. First, let me tell you what I can do for you," Peter began.

If nothing else, Cora was intrigued.

"I can let you know if this guy is good for you or not."

Cora smiled at him, and she knew she must look skeptical.

Peter held out his hands. "I know at first you're skeptical, but I want you to know I'm qualified. I've been in foster care since I was four. I'm fourteen and a half. I read in a book that if you've done something for ten years, you can say you're an expert. Well, for ten years I've been in different families, and I've watched all types of boyfriends, husbands, grandfathers and other men. I've seen the good and the bad. So while you are older than me. I think I have more experience."

She was speechless. Peter had just taken a piece of her heart. She was sure that wasn't his intention, and it wasn't what he was looking for. She cleared her throat and made sure to blink back the burning in her eyes, knowing that Peter wouldn't appreciate it.

"What is it that you want from me?" she asked softly.

Peter nodded and let out a breath. How simply a child saw things. Just because she was asking about her part, she could see that he thought she had bought into his expertise.

"The caseworkers take suggestions from the counselors here," Peter said as he looked intently at her. He swallowed a couple of times and bit his bottom lip when he wasn't talking. "I need you to recommend that Lili and I be split up."

"What? You're sister Lili?" Cora asked as she looked at him in confusion. "Peter, I don't understand?"

"Listen, you're right, you don't understand, but I have my reasons."

Cora shook her head. "No I don't think it works that way. You tell me what you want and I'll see if I can help you."

He stood up and paced for a moment, then stopped in front of her.

"Look Lili is getting older. I told you, I can help you know if he's a good guy because I've seen them both, good and bad guys. Lili and I have been lucky, but Lili can leave soon. Lili is going to be legal soon, so she can live on her own at 18. I don't want her to be around longer than she has too. I've seen some guys starting to look at Lili a little longer than I like."

"Have you told anyone? Have you told the caseworkers?"

"Nothing has happened and you can't report a person because you think they are bad. Our caseworkers are good, but they can't do anything until someone does something. You could help me protect Lili."

"Help protect Lili—"

Peter nodded. "The recommendation letter from you will go a long way."

"First, I think you'd need a letter from a veteran here. Michael would be the better person to get it from. Why didn't you ask Michael?"

Peter sat down. "I thought about it, but everyone says he's a crazy knight in shining armor. I need more time around him, and I don't have anyone I want to accuse."

"You'd be surprised by what he can do."

"I don't know…"

Cora shrugged her shoulders. "I have to ask, why did you pick me? I'm not a regular at the camp."

Peter turned to go to the door. Then he stopped and looked over his shoulder. Most mornings you go outside and you meditate. One time, you went out to meditate and you crushed a flower. I saw you come in here and get a bowl and then replant the remnants of the flower. I thought if she'll do that for a flower, she's the one who will help me."

Peter opened the door and tossed over his shoulder. "Think about what I said, and remember, I'm counting on you, Mrs. Thalman, because just like I can spot a good man, I know a good woman when I see one too."

Cora watched the door close and looked up at the ceiling so the tears wouldn't fall. She knew what she needed. She needed to take a quick meditation.

Ten

That man knew how to make an entrance. She hadn't seen him all morning during orientation, and now he was coming toward her sitting at a picnic bench outside. She ran her tongue over her teeth to make sure none of her seaweed wrap was still in there. *That's just what I need.*

When Michael moved, every muscle in his body moved with him. He was a walking piece of art. She used to tease him about how he kept fit. Who expected an architect to stay fit? He would always say people trusted his designs if he looked good as well.

She pulled her gaze from his body to his face. Her eyes fell to his lips, and the memory of their kiss came back.

"Cora," he said as he took a seat next to her. "Sorry I missed the morning session, I was getting some things together."

"I missed you."

She saw his eyebrow raise. Then she shook her head and gave a small laugh. "What I mean is, I wanted to talk to you about the kids we have and—"

"Ahh, we can talk about that if you want. I just came by to make sure you weren't isolating yourself during lunch," he said as he looked at her on the bench alone.

Cora paused and took stock of her solitary bench. He saw too much. He understood her too well. What was she thinking even going down this road? She knew where it was going. She could feel herself falling for this man all over again. It was the little tingles when he was in the vicinity. It was only a matter of time before she would have to admit that he had won.

When she got to that point, she'd have to trust him and herself to be together again. To love again. No matter how much they said they loved each, the fact of the matter was she couldn't have children anymore. Children were a big part of Michael's dream. Could he let go of that dream? Would she be enough?

She had told herself that she was going to come to his camp and find closure. Instead, she was at the camp, and she was finding that things weren't as black and white as she thought. She was finding that maybe she should have had more faith in them and...

She felt the warmth of Michael's hand on hers, and it startled her.

"Cora, your thoughts are going too fast. I can see your hair waving in the air."

"What?" she placed her hand on her hair to find it was just a light breeze that was ruffling her hair.

"You're doing what you normally do. You're trying to figure it all out and work on all the scenarios."

"Really?"

He sat down and covered her hand in his. "Really. In fact, I knew this would happen, and I came here with a plan to assist you."

Cora was skeptical, but a bit intrigued about what he would come up with as well. She looked at their hands and then pulled hers back.

"How are you going to help me?"

Michael chuckled. "Always the skeptic, it's one of the things that I admire about you Cora. I grew up with parents who were artists, so being emotional was a given. We moved first and thought second. With you, I always knew we'd be thinking first and moving second."

She looked away from him and at her hands. Of course, she knew about Michael's family. She had met his father before he passed.

She had thought her planning would be a negative. She couldn't stop planning, but she had never known Michael had admired the quality. She could feel the heat in her face and hoped the cool breeze would help.

"I've been working on this, and I want us to play together."

Cora looked up and saw Michael had a paper origami fortune teller in his hand. She hadn't seen one since she was in elementary school. It was made from a specifically folded sheet of paper, you could put your pointer and your thumb in the pockets and by opening and closing it, different numbers would show up, and questions were asked. She remembered how she played with it as a kid.

"I can see you remember what this is. I've fixed this one to be a little different. Instead of having yes and no, and numbers on it. It has a few questions. I thought it would help us. You know, as we get to know each other."

"Or we could do what other people do and just ask things we think are relevant?"

"Psh! And pass up having fun? Nope, we need to interject some fun into the reacquaintance, don't you think?"

"Fine. We'll play your game. What question do you have?"

"Pick a number and then we'll see what question the fortuneteller lands on," he said with a grin. The words didn't bring any comfort to her. Instead, they seemed to up her anxiety.

It was silly. There was no reason to indulge in his silliness, and yet she couldn't stop the word from leaving her mouth.

"Four."

He moved the storyteller four times and then pulled the flap open and read the question. "When did you last sing to yourself?"

She had been waiting for a strange question, but this wasn't it.

"When was the last time I sang to myself?"

Michael grinned. "Repeating the question isn't an answer."

She sighed. "Michael—"

"I happen to know you have a beautiful voice."

Cora looked at him and swallowed. "Do you?"

Michael nodded. "I remember you used to sing in the shower. It would always be something old but good. Sometimes you sang something from old Blue Eyes. Sometimes you just hummed classical, but you have a beautiful voice. I used to listen to it outside the bathroom and smile. Who would think the woman who could organize everything, could also sing the beast to sleep?"

Cora was speechless. How did he do it? She tried to give herself some time to digest what he had said. Then she remembered the last year and had to swallow back the heat of tears.

"I haven't sung in my shower since I lost Hope. Until you mentioned it right now, I had almost forgotten that I sang in the shower."

She shied away from him and took deep breaths to keep herself together. She nodded and then reached out and took the fortuneteller.

"Your turn, pick a number."

"Cora?"

She almost broke, hearing the concern in his voice. The low tone that beckoned her in to confide in him and rest on him. She shook it off.

"Pick a number, Michael. Just pick a number, please."

"Seven."

She moved the fortune teller and then tried to clear her throat. She put on a smile and opened up to the question.

"Okay, what would be a perfect day for you?"

She looked at Michael, and he smiled.

"My perfect day would be waking up to you singing in the shower. Meeting you in the office in the company we both dreamed about and built. Then I'd come home and you'd be waiting for me with Chinese food and a movie, that will undoubtedly make you cry. When it was done, we'd go to sleep in each other's arms. Yeah, Cora, I know the answer to this question, because I've been dreaming about that day every day since you left."

"I—"

Before she could say anything, someone called Michael, and he turned and waved to them.

"Cora, I'm sorry. We can pick up our game later," he said with a smile. He leaned over and kissed her on the forehead. He walked away and all Cora could do was watch him go. This man had been dreaming of her? It was almost too much for her to comprehend.

She and Michael were going to try it again. She was going to open herself to the joy, and the pain, of loving him again. What was she thinking? Even if it all went well, Michael was a loving person, and he would want children. He would want to build a family. She was here to see if she could be around children, but the idea of having them in a house with her and Michael, she couldn't imagine it.

Her breath was coming fast and she couldn't swallow enough to keep her throat dry. She'd tell him that she couldn't do this. If she was ever going to be with a man, it had to be with the one who wanted a relationship but not a family. She just had to figure out how to tell Michael.

Eleven

She hadn't been able to catch up with Michael. He hadn't shown up yet. She was sitting on her mat in front of her cabin, trying to find that calm space to settle into. Trying to leave behind the thoughts of facing Michael. When she opened her eyes, the sun had set, leaving a nice glow to fall all around the camp. In a couple of hours, dusk would come and the fireflies would come out. The sight of them brought her calm in a time when her soul was in such turmoil. She closed her eyes and took a deep breath, waiting to fall into calmness when it happened.

"What did Peter speak to you about?" Lili asked, suddenly in front of her. "What did he need to say to you that I couldn't be there?"

Cora opened her eyes and looked at the determined young woman. All vestiges of calmness left at that moment. Lili, on the other hand, was the epitome of a young warrior princess. She stood with her arms crossed over her chest. The white of her hands gave away how tense she was. Lili had on black jeans and a worn red and black plaid shirt that hung on her small frame. With piercing dark eyes that never wavered.

"He had some concerns and wanted to know if I would be giving a report," Cora said. "I can see you are concerned, but you need to tread carefully here Lili. I took the classes, but I was born in a different era when children learned to respect their elders and tone mattered."

Lili swallowed and took a hesitant step back. "I'm not trying to be rude. I just want to make sure he's okay."

Cora looked at Lili and saw beyond her bravado to the young woman who was here for her only family. She understood all too well what it meant to have family, and she had to admit that she would do anything for family as well. At the end of the day, wasn't that the reason Michael was here to fight? For the possibility of a family? She could tell Lili to go away, but she wouldn't.

"I don't know how okay Peter is, but I can tell that he loves you."

"He thinks he needs to take care of me and it's not true. I'm the older one and I need to take care of him." Lili said fiercely. "I know you all think we're just kids but my brother thinks he's bigger than he is sometimes. He doesn't understand that we have to play by the rules for a little while. I've got a plan if he could just be…" she trailed off with a whimper.

Cora had to swallow once again to keep herself together. "I understand how it is to love someone so much you'd do anything for them."

Lili stopped and gave Cora a small smile. "Maybe you do," she said sadly. Lili looked around the camp and then back at Cora. "This place. We've come here for three years. It's always a good time for us both to be able to talk without having to worry about our foster families listening in or looking for signs that something is wrong with us. This year, when we came here, Peter's been different."

Cora wasn't sure how, but she was going to help them. She would probably need Michael, but she was going to do her best to help them both.

"Men and boys can be unknowable sometimes," Cora said. "Tomorrow we meet, and we'll see how the day plays out. Okay?"

Lili paused and then nodded. "Okay, as long as we're clear. If you find out something about Peter that I should know, you'll tell me, right?"

Cora hesitated. "I'm new here. If I hear something, let me talk it over with Michael first," she said. "He brought me here. I don't want to break a rule, okay? And then I'll talk to you."

Lili hesitated, and Cora waited for the push back. "Is it because you all are trying to get back together?"

Cora rolled her eyes. "Does everyone know about Michael and me? We can't be that interesting."

Lili smiled. "He's focused."

"Uh-huh, is that what we're calling it?"

"He says he really loves you," Lili said wistfully.

"He does." *If only it was that simple,* Cora thought. "I don't know if that's enough."

"I hope it is," Lili said.

Cora frowned. "Why?"

"Because that's the only thing that I tell Peter keeps us together. When we found out we were coming, a sponsor threw a party for us. I think her name was Danvers."

Cora sighed. "I know her."

"She told me at the dinner that I should make sure I go to school and watch out for myself. That Peter would grow up just fine. She said boys love differently and have to leave anyway when they get a certain age, it's just the way they are. I nodded, but I knew what her problem was right then."

"And it was?"

"She had never been loved by anyone and she's never loved anyone back. Peter and I may not always agree, but we love each other no matter what. I'll see you the day after tomorrow."

"Why not tomorrow?"

Lili laughed. "It's the same every year before we all pair up. There's a fitness day. The kids do runs and we record the time. I think the counselors do the same. So not tomorrow. Peter loves the fitness day."

"Thanks. I'm sure it's on my schedule, I'm just taking a little longer getting into things here. So, until the day after tomorrow, then."

Lili smiled. "Get some rest, and drink lots of water."

Cora watched Lili walk away and thought it would be nice to be that confident, to be able to blindly trust in love like that. To be carefree. To take things the way they came and not hold on to the past but keep looking forward, like Lili and Peter did. She had been that way once, a long time ago.

It was the end of the day for the physical fitness check. Cora understood why they tried to put team building into the event by asking them to run together and do other activities. She didn't mind, but she had been looking for Michael all day long. Someone said that he'd had to address some issues and couldn't come to the event today. It was obviously a letdown for some of the other women in the group that he didn't put in an appearance. Cora smiled to herself. Knowing Michael, he probably didn't even notice how much his presence was appreciated.

It was time to get an early dinner, or late lunch, depending on how you were looking at it. Cora's stomach didn't care. Ben had been one of the people writing down the results for the day. He was standing on the outskirts of the group as the counselors broke up into groups, and others just went their own way. He looked up and pushed his glasses up on his nose and gave her a nod, and then began walking toward her.

She wasn't sure how she felt about Ben, but so far, the interaction hadn't been anything she wanted to further. Cora took a quick look around. There wasn't anyone around that she could enlist. There was enough going on during this camp for her to worry about the ticky-tacky politics that were everywhere. She turned back to see how close he was, and she jumped to discover him right in front of her.

"Well, it seems like the Thalmans were well represented here today," he said, tapping his clipboard.

"We are trying our best like everyone else."

"Well, I think that deserves a reward. I have to give in this clipboard, and then we can grab a bite from the main building. Tonight they'll be a prix fixe menu for everyone."

"Okay."

"Good, we can go right over," Ben said.

"Maybe I should go change and—"

"Don't be foolish, you're fine."

Cora had to hold her tongue. She plastered a smile on her face and stretched her neck. Ben walked up to someone, tapped them on the shoulder and then left the clipboard. Too soon, he was back and he extended his hand and guided her to the main house.

It was then that she saw Michael. He looked like he had just run over and was now clearly annoyed when he saw her with Ben. Ben cleared his throat. She nodded at Ben and then she gave Michael another glance. It was then that she thought maybe he was coming to see her and take her out. She just couldn't deal now. It was either drop everything and go off with Michael, which she definitely wasn't going to do or deal with Ben. She'd deal with Michael later. Right now, she had to deal with Ben, and no matter what he said she didn't think his motives were as innocent as he presented them to be.

She didn't bother talking to Ben as they went to the main house. She was trying to get that look on Michael's face out of her mind. He led her to a table in the back of the room. Cora felt like she was in one of those horror movies when the heroine was being led into a trap. Ben was a lot of things but subtle wasn't one of them. As soon as they were both sitting and he had waved to the wait staff going around taking orders, he smiled at Cora and began the interrogation.

"So, what is Michael up to these days?"

Cora looked over her shoulder, hoping that a waiter was on their way to their table. She didn't know what Ben wanted but she knew he wanted something. It seemed like there was a little more going on at the camp. All through the day, people had gone out their way to ask her one-off questions about Michael. She thought they were asking about them, but as the day wore on, she could tell there was something else they wanted to know. She just didn't know what it was.

"I guess he's preparing to start camp like we all are," Cora said, looking for a waitperson.

"Certainly he's talked about Glory Danvers' offer to help relocate this place," he said, with a smile that looked like it belonged on a shark and not a human.

"Ben, I'm not privy to what Michael is doing regardless of what people may think. I don't know anything, and I haven't asked him anything either. I'm here for the camp."

"Well, I guess. It's just that Danvers is offering a lot of money to relocate us. Everyone knows there was something going on there before you came."

"Hmm?"

"I keep telling Veronica, her son is a blue-collar worker and doesn't understand the goldmine that she's sitting on. I mean, it would be good for everyone if we relocated. The only person Veronica listens to beside her son, Cord, is Michael."

"It's been a year since Michael and I have been together, and I haven't been here. I think you all should talk it out like you've been doing for the last year."

"New Year and new people," Ben said. "The rumors are going through the camp that Danvers' offer is going to be flat-out refused."

"Michael has previous experience with Glory Danvers, and I'm sure he'll advise Veronica on doing what he thinks is the best thing. Michael has a good head on his shoulder."

"For someone who isn't with him and isn't planning on being with a him, you have a lot of faith in him."

"He's human and we all have faults. He might not even be the first person I'd let write up a proposal, but when it comes to planning, he's one of the best—if not the best—hands you could be in."

"In other words, you'd trust him with your future?"

Cora smiled and thought about what Ben had asked her. Would she trust Michael with her future? With their future? "Yes, I would."

Ben nodded. "Well, if you put it that way…"

Cora turned and raised her hand. "I don't know what's taking them so long. Oh look, a young lady is coming."

When Cora looked back at Ben, he looked a little anxious, looking at the young woman who was taking her sweet time coming to there table. His gaze went from the girl, to Cora as he pressed on. "Of course, of course, we should eat. They usually have a burger option, a vegan option and fish. The prix fixe is a reward for us all. I saw the roster; you have Peter and Lili."

"Yes, I do," Cora said, looking at the young woman who was detoured from coming to their table by someone else.

"You know how it can be when you're not in the inner circle and you aren't kept in the loop on everything. Veronica is looking at the offer from Danvers, and Danvers is making a big play if the rumors are true."

Still looking over her shoulder, she asked, "You think she's making a play?"

"Well, the number of Ms. Danvers' calls for Michael alone are enough to cause a ruckus. Oh, she says she's coming by to see the kids and the camp, but it's very apparent that she's here for Michael. The times she's driven here to pick him up and brought him back late. I mean, you can't help but hear him when she returns him. We all live around the main building. For a moment, I thought Michael was going to save the camp by hooking up with her," Ben laughed wryly.

Cora kept her face neutral, but her feelings were anything but. "You saw them together?"

Ben turned and looked at her with a wide smile. "Yes, he brought her to all the camp planning meetings. I'm a light sleeper. I was trying to get some warm milk to sleep, and Glory's red Porsche purred into the driveway."

Cora thought about Michael coming to her to look over the contracts. "It's odd Michael would ask me to help with contracts if he and Glory were on better terms."

"You know how those creative types are. They are so passionate, so it's off today, but on tomorrow."

The question and the mood were broken by the waitress who finally made it to the table. "Let me tell you the three options…"

Cora smiled and nodded. She couldn't tell which one she chose because all she could hear was that Michael had spent the last year with Glory. This meal couldn't end quick enough.

Twelve

Cora couldn't wait to leave Ben at the main house. She was a little nervous that he wanted to follow her back to the cabin to talk about Michael and his plans. *His plans with Glory if the rumors were to be believed,* she mimicked to herself. The whole evening had been a polite inquisition.

It made her wonder if everyone thought she would fall under Michael's spell of charisma and charm. She was well aware of the good and the bad about Michael. If any falling went on it would be because she had approved it. She shook herself mentally as she thought about the turmoil that Michael stirred up in her. The conversation with Ben just confirmed that she couldn't do this with Michael, no matter how many glimpses of a hopeful tomorrow she caught. She knew they were just that; glimpses of a dream.

She had settled her decision and knew it was the right thing to do, until she walked around the bend closer to her cabin and saw him sitting on the steps in front of her place.

"I'm glad that Ben didn't think you needed so much help that he had to walk you back to your cabin," Michael said in a low tone.

Cora gave him a cold reception and crossed her arms over her chest. He wasn't disturbed. In fact, he hadn't moved a muscle sitting on her stoop. His legs were extended and crossed as he waited for her.

"I'm at a loss as to why you're here," Cora said. She knew what she was going to do. She knew she had to tell him it wasn't going to work, but the rest of her was thrilled to see him. Her pulse had kicked up a notch. Her whole body had revved up, not sure what was about to happen, but prepared for anything. It was the effect Michael had on her. She dreaded it and loved it.

Michael looked up at her and then got to his feet. "I'm curious, did Ben invite you to eat with him or did you go with him to avoid me?"

Cora looked into his eyes and instead of seeing anger, she saw an anxiousness. "Michael, he invited me to the hall. I wouldn't do that. If I don't want to see you, I'll tell you. We're still friends and people who respect one another, right?"

He ran his hands through his hair and then nodded.

"I'm sorry, of course you're right. It's been stressful around here lately, and I was looking forward to being with you today."

"Michael, we've never played those games. I wouldn't start now. If I'm going to be completely transparent though, had I seen you earlier, I was going to tell you that I don't think we should do this, trying to get back together again."

"Well, I'm glad I dodged that. Maybe I should be thanking Ben instead."

"Michael—"

"Us not being together, that was a thought for you?"

"Ben told me about you and Glory. It's not just that either. It's everything."

"You are everything to me, Cora. Glory and I only have business between us."

"She's a beautiful woman, Michael, and you're not dead."

"I'm not dead, but I already have the most beautiful woman. She's beautiful inside and out."

"Michael, at the end of the day, you'd still want a family."

"And I'd have one. You."

Cora stilled. "Michael?"

"Listen, people all over the world are looking for that one. We found each other. We had a loss. A tragic loss but we still have each other. I know I'm not perfect Cora. I'm not going to tell you some story about how I'm going to change and become perfect. I respect you too much to feed you fairy tales. No matter what, there will always be honesty between us. I think what we have is worth fighting for, but I need you to be all in for it to work."

Cora looked at him, and a feeling was spreading through her that was leaving her breathless and anxious. She was the rational one. She was the logical one. However, this feeling running through her was a sign. She knew everything that Michael said was true. If she did the safe thing, she'd walk away right now. If she did that, she knew she'd regret not taking this path. It was then that she made her decision.

"I'm in."

Michael held out his hand, and Cora looked at it, confused.

Michael's smile spread across his face, and he stepped toward her as she lay her hand in his. His smile promised secrets and magic that she could only imagine. They were close enough that she knew he would be able to tell she was breathless. She wouldn't step back, it wasn't her way.

"Michael?"

"A dance to celebrate, nothing more. Give me this Cora, please."

When she felt his arm go around her waist, her body came alive and her already committed heart began to sing. This was the feeling that she had been missing for the last year. She felt out of control, free and loved. She laughed.

"Was that a laugh? A lesser man might have an issue, but because I'm secure in myself, I can ask. What's so funny?" He whispered the words on the side of her neck, and they sank into her as the heat of his breath warmed her.

"Maybe it was a laugh." Cora leaned a little more in to him. " Should I tell you what I'm thinking? I'm not so sure."

"Remember, no secrets, tell me," he said as his lips brushed against her ear lobe.

"I was thinking that from all that time together, I may have picked up some of your more spontaneous reactions."

"I take whatever help I can get."

"You would."

"I'm shameless, Cora. This is all about you and me." He began to sway from side to side and she moved with him. Just when she thought he couldn't make the moment any sweeter, he leaned down and placed a kiss right behind her ear.

Cora took a deep breath. When had that spot become so sensitive? Her hand tightened on his shoulder and he pulled back to bring her fingertips to his lips.

"I dreamed this so many nights. Now that you're here, I don't want to let you go. I might wake up."

"I'm here, Michael."

"This is how it's supposed to be." Michael leaned down until they were head to head.

Then a voice made them both jump.

"Ms. Thalman, are you okay?" Peter called out.

Michael groaned, lifted his head and then looked back at Cora.

"It seems you have a guardian angel looking out for you, Cora."

She smiled nervously. Cora could feel Michael's body holding her protectively. She knew it was about to end, but she held on to the moment as long as she could. Cora laid her head on his chest and heard his heart beating strong and rapidly. She let her smile spread across her face. She wasn't in this alone.

"Peter, we're fine," Michael called out.

"I hear you, Mr. Thalman, but I'm going to have to hear it from Ms. Thalman. If you could just release her."

Cora laughed in Michael's chest as she heard Peter. She knew he was taking their deal seriously. She looked up to see the incredulous look on Michael's face and stepped back. Turning around, she faced Peter.

"Hi, Peter. Thanks for coming by. It turns out that Michael is just leaving."

"I am?" whispered Michael for her ears only.

"Michael can take you back to your cabin. Thanks for coming out," Cora said before turning to face Michael. "Don't hurt my guardian angel's feelings. I'm here Michael. We have time."

Michael nodded. He began to lean down, but then Cora cleared her throat.

"Umm… Peter is watching."

"Seriously?"

Cora smiled. "Good night, Michael." She patted him on the chest and went into her cabin. She didn't turn around. She could tell from the deep breathing and the way Michael murmured loudly, "I can't believe this," that it was going to be okay.

Thirteen

Michael couldn't have asked for a better morning. The sun was out. Things were moving in the right direction with him and Cora. Michael picked up Cora, and they met Peter and Lili in the main cabin for breakfast. Afterward, the groups broke out and they were told the theme this year was Home. There were several treehouses that had been built already, and the kids would get to pick them out. Then counselors would make renovations or additions as needed according to their skill set. The goal was to give the foster kids an opportunity to create what they thought home should be.

It was one of many exercises, and it allowed the counselors to follow their charges through the forest as they looked at each house and then chose one. Michael was pretty sure Peter and Lili were going to choose a treehouse that was more of a cabin than a treehouse. It was one of the options for the children who didn't like heights. As the kids went through with their checklist and built a shopping list, it gave Michael time with Cora.

They sat on a portable bench that had been put in front of the treehouse. Michael was relaxing with his arm around Cora's shoulders. Several times she had moved closer to him, and it brought a sense of peace that Michael had been missing for a year. As he watched Peter and Lili, there was something that was bothering him.

"Cora?"

"Yes"

"You called Peter, your guardian angel. When did that happen?"

She sighed. "It was part of the deal he made with me."

"A deal?"

He felt her body stiffen and she pulled back to look at him. Her hand went to her mouth.

"I was going to tell you."

"Tell me what?"

"Peter wants me to write up a report that will separate him and Lili."

"What?" he said a bit sharply. "Why would he want that and why would he ask you? I'll just—"

Cora grabbed him by the shirt and pulled him back. "Michael, listen to me."

"Listen?" he asked, incredulous as he put his hands over hers. "It's not ethical. He knows better and I can't believe he put you in a position like that."

"Think about how desperate he needed to be to ask a stranger! Think about him, not me."

He looked into her eyes and took a deep breath. She was right. He only thought about how his compassionate, loving Cora would have felt and he thought only to protect her.

"He's concerned that Lili is getting older and that he can't protect her," Cora whispered.

All of the fight went out of Michael when he heard Cora's words. "Have there been any incidents that—"

Cora shook her head. "No, I asked the same thing. He's just cautious. He doesn't have anything to report, and he said the caseworkers are good, but something has to happen in order to report. He just wants to protect Lili."

Michael sighed. "I would think them being together would be best—"

"Peter doesn't want to be used against her and he wants Lili to leave as soon as she can. He thinks if they are together that won't happen."

"It's a rough spot. So many foster kids and not enough families. It's hard for agencies to police. Hard on foster kids being moved. Such a great need and not enough help."

Cora cleared her throat and looked down at her lap as if there was something very interesting there.

"I knew once you heard the issue, you would agree it's a problem."

"Uh-huh," Michael replied. Still Cora hadn't looked at him. He reached out and placed his finger under her chin and lifted it up until he could see her eyes. They were bright and guilty. "Umm, Cora, is there something else you want to say?"

"I knew you'd see this was a problem."

"Uh-huh…"

"So I had a plan."

"A plan?"

"What are you going to do, fix foster care in the U.S.?"

"No, silly, that would take way too much time. I thought I needed a creative person to help out on this."

"A creative—"

"Wait for it."

"Cora—"

"Listen, I think we can figure out most things if we put our heads together."

"So you think I can come up with a fix for Peter and Lili?"

"I do."

"They aren't the only ones with this kind of problem, Cora."

She reached out and placed her hand on his cheek. "I know Michael. But for now they are ours. We need to think of something. We have to do something to help them."

"Cora I know this is close to home for you because of Ho—"

She placed her fingertips over his mouth. "We'll find a way."

Fourteen

Part of the purpose of the camp was to create alone time for each child, and that was where Michael found himself this morning. He had been thinking about it all night after Cora had told him about Peter. He knew that this was a part of Cora's nature. Michael knew she thought herself to be cold and removed but Michael knew better. Underneath, Cora was the cheerleader for the underdog. She was the one who gave a dollar to anyone who asked.

Michael had decided to talk to Peter first and then figure out what could be done. Peter came to him hesitantly, looking around before he stopped in front of him. Why hadn't he noticed that before?

"Hi, I wasn't sure if you really wanted to meet up today, alone."

Michael's protective instincts started to flare when he heard the hesitancy in the child's voice. He groaned to himself. He wasn't sure what was going to happen, but Cora was right, he would find an answer.

"We're alone and we need to talk."

"Okay," Peter said with a shrug. The boy's hair was still wet and his shirt was wrinkled. It brought a grin to

Michael's face. Peter probably woke up at the last moment and then ran through his clothes picking up the first thing he could find. He remembered those days.

"I brought lunch. Let's sit on the bench."

Michael had already laid out two bags with sandwiches on the picnic table.

"I spoke with Cora."

Peter stopped and then nodded. "So she told you?"

"She said you made a deal with her, in exchange for her evaluation."

Peter nodded. "I did, you gonna send me back to my foster home now?"

Michael looked at Peter, all unrepentant. "Is there a problem with your foster home?"

Peter shook his head. "This home is real good, but we heard that the wife is sick. He's not going to be able to keep us. We understand, and we'll have to see how it goes."

Michael stopped. "I didn't know."

"Yeah, they told us before we came."

"So why did you want Cora?"

Peter looked up and Michael could see him blinking quickly. "It took a while to find a family that would take us both. Lili will have a better chance with a good family and good people, without me. People think boys are trouble you know?"

"Peter, you're no trouble."

"Not now but sometimes things happen," Peter muttered. "Lili does everything for me, but I saw a couple of the other families. Some of the people who came weren't too good for her."

"Let's eat."

Peter looked confused. "Let's eat? That's all you have to say?!"

Michael opened up his bag and took out his sandwich. "I'm a little older than you Peter. I need food, and besides, I have an idea, but it's so crazy I have to think about it."

"Well, what is it?" Peter asked.

Michael shook his head. "I need to figure it all out. Let's eat and then we can meet up with the girls this afternoon. For now though let's keep this talk between us."

Peter still looked confused.

"Stop thinking so hard. The answer will come."

"Who said that?" Peter asked.

"I did, now eat."

Michael looked at Peter and thought about what he'd said. He chewed his food and looked at Peter. The thought was madness. It was crazy enough to be possible.

Cora sat in front of the pottery cabin. She was transfixed by a mug that was shaped like a young woman sitting cross-legged, holding her arm off to the side. The young woman had her hand on her hip in a sassy pose, and the arm served as the handle. The display was setup outside of the cabin Cora supposed to mark this one as a potters cabin and to show off the pieces.

It was one of the many pieces in the cabin that had been made by visitors to the camp. However, the skill that was shown in this particular piece could be attributed to Melinda. She was surprised to find the project manager's hobby was pottery. All the pottery was displayed on shelves and racks, which made the place look like a store. Cora walked around the room, touching items that caught her fancy until she heard the door open.

"You're early, but no matter," Melinda said with her clipboard in her hand. "I'm glad you were able to get away from Michael, period."

"I have to be back at my cabin shortly. I'm a little confused about why you called me Melinda?"

"It's no secret. The camp has been offered by a realtor to move. The new space isn't all it's supposed to be. I've been doing the best that I can answering the mail around here, but I think it would be easier if I could have a sit-down with Veronica."

Cora shrugged and nodded in agreement. "Okay and…"

"Veronica is doing other things and had delegated these items to Michael. Michael is doing things but he's not really sharing and that puts all of us on edge."

Cora shook her head. "I can see how this is a problem but why—?"

"Why did I want to talk to you? Because Michael listens to you. He isn't neglecting his duties; I just think he's not taking any time to express what the decisions from those duties are either."

"You're dealing with Ms. Danvers. Have you tried that route? Talking to them? I've seen the contract, and any of you can go talk to her about the arrangements or how she is involved with the movement of the camp."

Melinda peered at her. "Please, please, please tell me you are not upset because we're dealing with Glory Danvers? I know it seemed like there was something going on between Michael and Glory, but since you're here I think it's safe to say that whatever we thought was going on, is over."

"It seems that way," Cora agreed.

"You know Michael. He's always looking for the best way to handle a situation. When the situation isn't architecture and/or drawing, his go-to is to find someone else to help handle it."

Cora sighed. She completely understood Melinda's words since she had also been a witness to him trying to give away situations he wasn't comfortable with.

"So I have an idea," Melinda said.

Cora never liked it when other people came up with ideas. Nine times out of ten, it didn't bode well for her.

"I think you should talk to Michael about this or take care of Danvers."

Cora stopped for a moment and then laughed. "I think you just asked me to reign in Michael, and anyone who knows him, knows that is a long shot at best."

"Well, Michael says you're really good at reading contracts. Maybe you could find something in them to help us."

"As you pointed out earlier, Danvers and I have crossed paths once or twice. I might make this situation worse."

Melinda sighed. "I think it's getting close to a critical point so I probably wouldn't worry about that. I know it's a lot, I just wanted to know if you'd try. Veronica has blind faith in Michael and without him communicating to everyone…"

Cora nodded and held up her hands in surrender. "I'll try. I'm not making any promises, but I'll try."

"Thanks. Also, I want to talk about Lili." Melinda had her arms crossed over her chest. "I've been in contact with the counselor and everyone is very worried about her."

"I was with Lili earlier and she seemed fine. Maybe she was a bit distracted but that was it."

Melinda sighed. "It just means she's good at hiding issues. Her counselor told us that she might be moving from the foster home she's in. We know she was very happy there and the couple had taken in both her and Peter. It's always a challenge to place two."

Cora frowned, thinking how adamant Peter was. Now it was beginning to make some sense. It just meant she really needed to get together with Michael and figure something out.

"Foster care is overburdened. It suffers all of the problems that well-meaning agencies are facing today. There is a huge demand but not enough people to help."

"I knew but I have to say being here at the camp brings it home in a very personal way. I need to think on this but I want to thank you for sharing with me. Regardless of what you may think of me or Michael I hope you know we only want the best for Peter and Lili," Cora said.

Fifteen

Cora wished she could see what the others saw. As it stood now she and Michael were together, but she couldn't just wave a wand and have Michael do whatever she wanted. Cora smoothed her hands over her floral dress. She wasn't sure what to wear, because when she asked Michael, he had said to make sure she was wearing comfortable clothing for their outing tonight. She picked up her purse and looked down to make sure her brown strap-on sandles were tied, and then she opened the door.

A black limo parked in front of her door. Cora poked her head out the cabin door and looked both ways. There were no plethora of limos in camp. In fact, she had expected to see a jeep or a truck show up, not a limousine. Okay, it must be someone on their way to their honeymoon maybe, and they were going through the camp. It was a nice area. She knew of a couple spots that a person might go to relax and have a special moment. If she were honest with herself, she'd admit that the reason she agreed to come to the camp was because it was close to her favorite bed and breakfast.

She figured she'd stop by there when the camp was over.

Before his body had cleared the door, she recognized Evan, all dressed up as a chauffeur. He stepped out, gave Cora a nod, and then opened up the door to the backseat and gestured for her to get in. When she tried to ask Evan what was going on, but he just smiled. Cora got into the car and the smell of rose petals enveloped her. Petals were strewn all over the backseat and on the floor. She couldn't move without crushing some petals and releasing even more of the relaxing smell of roses. There was a small pull out table that had a can of seltzer in a mug. Next to, it was a note. I remembered you don't really like to drink. Here's something that can still whet your whistle. The ride is about an hour but I assure you it's worth the wait and whatt's at the end of the ride will help you remember us.

An hour later Evan opened up the door and she stepped out in front of the Blue Dragon Bed and Breakfast. It was the same place she and Michael had gone to after their wedding. They had only stayed a night but it was everything she loved. In a lot of ways they had built their ideas of what a home should be form this place. You could look around the house and see their dreams. When Cora and Michael had bought their first house, they had patterned it after the bed and breakfast. The house had been decorated in blues and yellows, and lots of flowers. They had even decorated the lawn with blue and yellow flowers as a tribute to the time that they had spent here.

As she walked through the doors she expected to see the older couple, instead a young woman greeted her and said her parents no longer ran the B&B, she and her husband did. It was then that Cora realized, you could go back, but that didn't mean that things stayed the same.

They gave her a key to the room down the hall. When she opened the door, there Michael stood, by the windows, pouring strawberry soda into wine glasses.

"I wanted to be as authentic as possible," Michael said, putting the plastic soda bottle down.

Cora stepped into the room and tried not to laugh aloud.

"I'm surprised, you got the same soda we drank. Are we tempting fate?"

"No, we are reveling in our youthful ignorance. Can you believe we actually had the conversation of if standing in front of the microwave would make me infertile?

Cora looked around and found that the room had some cosmetic changes but it essentially looked the same way it did all those years ago when they came here for their honeymoon. She knew Michael was intent on bringing back what they had by reliving those days, but she had to admit, this was more than she expected. She had already said she would give them another try.

Being back in this room made her more nervous than she wanted to admit. It brought back the initial fear that came with coming to this room. When they had come the last time they were sure they were starting a brand new life together. Now they were here again and Michael thought they could start over again. She wasn't sure if maybe this meetup was a jinx on the new start they were trying. When she thought about how open Michael and she were now, it was a bit scarier. Looking around the room with everything sinking in; she wanted to run.

He picked up the fluted plastic cup and gave it to her. Then he picked up her hand and guided her to the loveseat. When she sat down the memories came back to her in waves. The two of them on the sofa. Him giving her a fluted glass and then the both of them with their heads together, and she confessing to him that she was sure this would last forever.

Now when she sat on this sofa, it had become a day of reckoning. She could just get up and leave. She could decide not to participate in this farce and let it all go. She wanted to but she couldn't, she wouldn't run. She took a deep breath and then took a healthy sip of her strawberry soda.

She winced. It was just as sweet as she remembered it. Cora was still shocked that the brand was still around. He didn't have to wine and dine her. She had already said yes.

She looked at him, confused. "Why all of this?"

"All of this is where we began. I don't think we started wrong. I think at some point, we just stopped talking, and then it went off track."

"Well, I'll give you this, it was romantic in its day…and today."

"I see I'm going to have to fight for every compliment."

"I'm here. Don't I get credit for that?"

"You do. Maybe you want to tell me all the sweet things we said in this room?"

Cora looked at him with a raised eyebrow.

"Are you sure you are remembering everything correctly?"

He smiled. "Of course, I told you, you were the most beautiful woman I'd ever met."

"You told me I would win against a Botticelli any day of the year."

He laughed and moved closer to her and put his arm around the back of the sofa. Cora looked at his arm.

"That is so high school."

"You were always quick. Personally, my thought is that oldies but goodies still work. I just want to be close to you."

Cora's back was stiff until she heard him speak and then she relaxed against the back of the sofa. The heat radiated from his arm, enticing her to sit back into the warmth and relax. This was Michael; she could lean back for a moment.

"Oldie, huh? Didn't anyone tell you never to bring up age when you're around a woman?"

"Really? I have to mention age because I'm not that spring chicken anymore."

"I think you still have a couple of good years in you," she joked.

He looked up at her and scooted a little closer before saying. "You think so?"

"Stop fishing for compliments. You're an attractive man and anyone would be happy to have you."

"Even you?"

"Yes, Michael, even me."

He turned to her and paused before his head began to lower. Just before his lips touched hers, he paused again.

"Are you ready, Cora?"

Cora nodded. She was waiting with bated breath, her heart thudding so loud that she would have sworn it was the only thing that could be heard in the room. One moment they had been sharing each other's breath, and then she was lost in the feel of his mouth moving on hers. Her doubts were fading away. This had always been the easy part with Michael. The kiss was just like Michael promised, it teased and wrapped around her, making her feel as though this would never end.

The heat radiating from her core seemed to grow with each beat of her heart. She shifted to lean into him a little closer and her hand rested on his shoulder. She could feel the contractions of his shoulder, and it helped to lull her even deeper into the moment since she knew she wasn't alone. This was them. His muscles flexed under her hand and just as she felt him shift, she thought he was about to move closer, and then he pulled back from the kiss and stood up. She waited for him to offer his hand and then pull her into his arms, but it never happened. Instead, he walked away and went to the food cart in the room.

She looked to him and waited to expectantly. "What are you doing?"

Michael held up his hand and then took his phone out. He sent a text and then let out a big breath.

"I'm getting some dessert, and I've called Evan to take you back."

"Take me back?" First, it was a wave of hurt and betrayal that flooded her. Then the feelings turned to anger.

"Yes, I think it's time to take you back."

Cora looked at him, the passion she felt fueled her anger as she shook her head. "Michael, what's going on here?"

He ran his hands through his hair.

"Cora, this attraction between the both of us has never been our problem. I've thought of leading with our attraction to each other, then working out the rest, but I made a discovery when we lost Hope. This isn't enough to get us through the hard times. It's good when things are good, but it's useless when we're hurting."

The anger drained out of her, and she closed her eyes. "It bites when you're right."

"I have to be right sometimes, right?"

"Why aren't you coming back with us? I mean, there's plenty of space in the limo."

"No, I need to make sure I'm staying on track as well. We have tomorrow."

A knock on the door made them both jump. After a nervous laugh he opened the door, and Evan stepped in.

Evan looked at both parties. "Are we good here?"

Cora smiled. "We're good."

"Then your chariot awaits," Evan said.

"It's been a pleasure, Cora."

Michael walked over, placed a kiss on her forehead, and then gave her a shaky smile.

"For what it's worth, the kiss on the forehead is because I don't trust myself any closer to your lips."

"Dude! I'm here, please!" Evan moaned.

Cora peeked around Michael and laughed. Then she gave Michael one last look. "Until tomorrow."

In the car, she thought about the night. Hope would never be forgotten, but tonight Michael showed her that there was a chance that love could go on. She didn't have to live in that moment or the guilt of the past. Michael showed her that it was possible to heal, and to make new memories in the place of old ones.

Sixteen

"Peter and Lili deserve better than this uncertainty they are facing," Michael said as he ate lunch with Veronica. "They're good kids. It's just not fair the way it's all falling out. It's even worse that we have to wait for something to happen."

Michael had met up with Peter, Lili, and Cora while they picked out rooms in the treehouse. The morning had been filled with getting to know everyone's taste as well as them sharing what they thought home was like and how the future could look. He knew this afternoon would be the continuation of them growing together.

Veronica picked up her coffee cup. "It could be that nothing happens at all. You know the reason I do this is because there aren't enough opportunities for foster care children. The system is overburdened, and the ones paying for it are the children and the caseworkers."

Michael bit into his hero sandwich and then noticed that Veronica only had some chips and hummus. "Did you forget lunch?"

Veronica laughed. "No, it's just the first time we've eaten at the same time. I don't think I could eat even half of what you're about to consume."

"It's all brain food, so I'm okay," Michael laughed.

"You seem more involved this year."

Michael finished eating the bite of hero he had in his mouth. "More involved?"

"Every year we serve these kids. This isn't your first year, but it is the first year that you've been so personally involved with the kids. I'm telling you to be careful Michael. I know you. You wear your heart on your sleeve even if everyone doesn't see it. The other part is the kids here are looking for hope, don't promise more than you can deliver," she said in a warning voice.

"I'm not more involved. I've always cared about the kids," Michael replied.

"I'm not saying you've been uninvolved. What I'm saying is you seem to be thinking more about having kids in your life and giving it the kind of thought that is influencing your future life decisions, and I can't help but think it has something to do with the fact that you happen to be trying to get your wife back."

"We're working on things, and I think we may be able to get through our history."

"You're on the same team with two children. This is not a house, Michael. There are lives involved here besides you and Cora."

"Cora can't have kids."

"Well, that does put a different spin on things for you doesn't it. I mean we know you having a big family has always been a part of the vision for you," Veronica said in a low voice.

"I've been thinking. I don't believe either Michael one of us has given up on the idea of family. We have to consider a different kind of family."

Veronica stopped and looked hard at. "This isn't going to be just about you two anymore. I can see where your thoughts are going to, and I'm telling you deciding to be a foster family is a group thing, not a solitary decision. This is not something you can wing it as you go."

"I'm taking it slow, Veronica."

"Think turtle-and-snail slow. I am so happy that you and Cora are finding yourselves. I think it's even better if the experiences you two are having here with the foster kids will help you to realize that you have other options. However, kids have a way of getting under your skin. They can weave themselves into the fabric of your life before you know it. I tell you this because Peter and Lili have a home. You can't be sure Cora wants foster kids, and even if she does, will she want two?"

"You can't fault me for considering it though."

Veronica smiled. "Michael, don't start lying to yourself now. You are doing more than considering it."

"I'll be careful."

"Famous last words of every child."

Michael valued Veronica's opinion, and right now was not the time to be anything but brutally honest about what he wanted. Michael wanted it all, and he thought it might be possible for him to get it.

He had a lot on his mind but the moment he saw them all working on the treehouse, all the doubt he thought he had melted away. He knew what he was going to do, and he knew it was going to work.

Seventeen

Cora felt as though she had been called to the principal's office. Yesterday, Michael, herself, and the kids had spent the day getting the home together. It was scary, but at the same time it was liberating. In the end, the treehouse reflected all of them cumulatively. Last night she had gone to sleep, and for the first time in a while, she hadn't had any dreams and hadn't gotten up in the middle of the night.

Then a spry Evan knocked on the door with a muffin in his hand.

"Veronica would like to have breakfast with you today before you start with the group."

That was how Cora found herself sitting across from the proverbial principal. The upside was that Veronica had a smile on her face. Now if only she knew how Veronica delivered her news, then she'd feel better. The downside was that Veronica looked as though she had something to get off of her chest, so she was going to find out soon enough.

"I spoke with Michael at lunch. I wanted to know how things were moving along. I'm sure that you've heard by now, as has everyone else, that Peter and Lili's foster parents are having a health crisis, and as a result, Peter and Lili won't be able to stay with them."

Cora sighed sadly. It was harder and harder to work with them and see what they thought family could be while knowing they were on the brink of losing everything they had that represented family.

"It's not definitive from what I hear. I'm praying that something will work out."

Veronica harrumphed. "I'm a bit too old to be betting on hopes and dreams. I prepare for the worst, and I'm pleasantly surprised when it doesn't come."

"Well, that is one way of doing it," Cora conceded.

"So the question is what will happen if it does come true? If it happens that they need to be rehomed. I have to ask you a question Cora, and I'd appreciate it if you could be honest."

"Please, feel free." Cora took controlled breaths and sat back in her chair. She wasn't sure what was about to be asked, but she wanted to make sure she didn't squeak the answer.

"You and Michael seem to be moving along, and I have no doubt that you two would and could make it as a couple. The question is, what about the family?"

Cora had to blink and look around because the question gut-punched her.

"Family?"

"Yes dear, family? I know I'm being forward, and you can tell me it's not of my business, and I won't be offended."

"No, I know you are important to Michael and I don't want to cut him off from those who would be there to support him," she said cautiously. "I think you're right; we have no problems as a couple. Family is the crux, right? Until I came here, I wasn't sure how I would feel about having a family that was ready-made, but this camp has opened my eyes."

"Well, that's good. I know he's putting a lot into this, and I want to make sure we are all open."

Cora cleared her throat. "If you don't mind, I'd like to ask some questions?"

Veronica's eyebrow went up, but she smiled. "Please do."

"I'm assuming that Michael has told you about my condition and what I did after our loss?"

"He did."

"I suppose he did that because you are close, but I need to talk to him about it. I want to make sure that Michael and I are having a conversation and not Michael, you and me. No disrespect, but there should be some things that are discussed between us before he discloses them."

Veronica nodded. "You've got the right of it, but don't be too hard on the boy. He's desperate to make sure everything goes okay between the two of you."

Cora thought on her words before she spoke.

"I hear you. I want to be just as clear with you as you have been with me today. I know there is an issue of what we will do about a family. Michael has said I'm enough, but I think this camp has made us realize that we both want something more.

"I have grown very fond of Peter and Lili. The daily interaction makes it impossible to not grow fond of them. It pains me that they have the concerns they have, and I have been thinking about Lili and Peter's issue. I was thinking about leaving my name and number for their caseworkers so they can get in contact with me."

"And Michael?"

"I can't ask Michael to do something like this. This is something that we have to take one step at a time."

Veronica started laughing, and Cora sat, confused. "I'm sorry—?"

Veronica held up her hand. "You have to forgive this old woman but you two are entirely too much alike. I thought that maybe Michael was being too forward and that he was pushing you too much being in this environment with children and trying to woo you, but what do I find? You are doing just fine with the wooing, and you're making your own plan when it comes to the children as well. I thought you two needed a mediator, but I find that you don't."

Cora smiled. "I have to say we're past that stage. I think what we need is a contract, though."

"A contract?"

"I know it sounds odd, but I think that would clear up all the rest of our issues that we have. If we put it in black and white."

Veronica smiled. "I wish I could be a fly on the wall when you present that idea to him."

Michael had received an invite to dinner but so had Evan. He thought maybe Cora wanted to thank them both for the trip to the bed and breakfast. It wasn't going to be the romantic thing he had imagined, but this was a part of who Cora was so he would eat with Evan, the human compactor.

As they walked over Michael looked over at the smiling Evan. "Listen, I think you should eat and then leave as early as possible. No staying until the last drop is gone."

Evan put his hand to his chest in mock horror. "Are you suggesting I should offend her by not eating everything she's made?"

Michael let out a long-suffering sigh and gave up on trying to convince Evan to leave early. As soon as they had both received the invite, Evan had made sure that he didn't eat as much lunch so he could do justice to Cora's meal.

Michael knew that Evan was just ribbing him. Evan was a good friend who had listened to him when he was in the land of woe. To see him smiling next to him as if it were Christmas was par for the course of them being friends.

When they got to the door, Evan reached it first and knocked. Cora opened the door, and Evan stepped in and hugged her.

"Cora, a woman who is after my heart and has found the path," Evan said dramatically. When he pulled back, Cora laughed.

"I'm not after your heart, but I did want your body to be here, and I knew this was the way to make sure it showed up."

Evan nodded. "You were right. Is dinner done?" he asked expectantly.

"Yes, gentlemen, please come in. Everything is ready for you." Michael shrugged his shoulders as he walked past Cora.

"I'm going to wash my hands," Evan said and disappeared to the back.

"I'm glad you made it," Cora said to Michael.

"Evan would have deadlifted me to get me here. The only thing he heard was a home-cooked meal and that he didn't have to eat in the main building, and he was on his way."

Cora smirked. "I said I'd make dinner. I didn't say I'd feed an army of one."

"Is there a reason you invited Evan?" Michael asked.

"I'll need him later. Right now, let's eat and then the rest will be clear."

An hour later, Michael watched Evan sit back in his chair, rubbing his belly like a contented cat.

"Any doggy bags you want me to take?"

Cora raised her brow and looked at Evan. "No, there is no doggy bag, but it's time for you to earn your meal."

"Earn my meal? It had a price?"

Michael waited. "Okay, Cora."

She smiled. "I think that we need a contract."

Evan looked between them. "A contract? I need to leave."

Cora reached out and stopped him. "No, you don't, because you're the witness."

Evan shook his head. "Oh, I don't know—"

Michael smiled. "Stay Evan. Go for it."

Cora pulled out a paper and put it on the table. "Let's negotiate."

Michael pulled it toward him. "I'm listening and reading."

"To start, we should always discuss if we are going to tell other people our personal business," Cora said.

Michael nodded. Cora produced a pen, and Michael checked off a line on his copy.

"We should keep Thalman Designs. All decisions regarding contracts from here on will be mine, and designs will be yours."

"Thank goodness," Michael said.

"We know we want a family, and we have to be open to all alternatives."

"Done!"

"We decide together on all items that affect us both. I should have let you know before I made that decision to see the doctor."

Michael swallowed and nodded. "I want to tell you I understand, but I don't really. We both dealt with losing Hope in different ways. I certainly didn't tell you how I beat myself up, so I'll tell you what I hope I'll get in return from you. I accept whatever decisions you made, and I support them."

"Done," she whispered.

Evan cleared his throat and looked between the both of them. "I want you to know that this was really uncomfortable, but now that I've survived, I can say it was definitely worth the food. So do you both cut your palms and do a blood oath or something?"

Cora turned toward Evan. "No, we don't. His word is good enough. I've got dessert for everyone unless you feel like you want to leave now Evan?"

Evan smiled and then nudged Michael in the side. "Michael knows I always have room for dessert."

Michael rolled his eyes and then gazed at Cora. He wasn't sure what was going to happen tonight. In fact, he thought Cora was trying to push him away, but now that she was serving slices of red velvet cake, he felt as though he was one step closer to his goal.

When the cake was done and then they were headed to the door, Evan was waved as he went out. Michael turned, leaned down, and gave Cora a kiss before she knew what was going on.

"Thanks, Cora."

He saw her turn away as a blush appeared on her cheeks.

"We've been married, been through so much and you still blush? You are a mystery to me, sometimes Cora."

She pushed him out the door. "It's a mystery to you because you have no shame," she laughed. "Go, I'll see you tomorrow."

Eighteen

Cora opened the door to go to breakfast, and Melinda was standing outside, looking harried and worried.

"I'm so glad you're here," Melinda said breathlessly.

Cora watched as Melinda came into her cabin, and looked back outside.

"Oh well, I guess breakfast is just not going to be a thing for me today," Cora mumbled. "What's wrong?" Cora asked as she went to follow Melinda to the couch.

"I've been trying to manage a situation, but it's going downhill. I haven't told Veronica, because I told her once and she wasn't very moved but I think things are different now."

"Hold up, go back, and tell me from the beginning."

"A company called Enterprise has been sending warrants to the school."

"When did that start?" Cora asked.

"It started with legal letters but Veronica said they were nothing. Some of them had Danvers on it so I know Michael gave it to Glory, and she was going to fix it. I want to say it did stop for a minute but now it seems like it's back again."

"Who else knows besides you?" Cora asked.

"Ben does. He's been trying to help me find a lawyer who can help. He had found a person who seemed like they were doing the right thing, but then they left."

"Okay, Melinda, let's see if we can find Ben. I've got to let Michael know—"

Melinda was already pulling out her phone. "I'll text Evan, and he'll explain it to him so we can go talk to Ben."

With that, Cora went with Melinda wondering if the day could get any more complicated.

"You mean she didn't tell you where she was going? It's not like her to miss out with the kids," Michael said to Evan.

"Listen, I got a text from Melinda saying she was going to take care of some business with Cora and that I should tell you that you are riding shotgun with the kids today."

Michael had already texted Cora and she hadn't answered. He knew about the realtors wanting to give Veronica a better price. He hadn't been able to talk to Glory since Cora arrived and somehow, she had found out that Cora was on camp and had stopped taking his calls.

Michael watched as Evan left the cabin and then he paced trying to calm himself down. He had some contacts look into the realty company that had been making the offer to Veronica. They didn't have a great reputation. In fact, there were some of his contacts that said the group was shady. His friend Lionel Chase was paranoid about everyone but Michael supposed that was why Lionel was a billionaire. Lionel was the first person he had reached out to about the company. Michael recalled the conversation Lionel, and he had on the phone just this morning.

"You're sure Glory Danvers is part of the same company trying to buy the land?" Michael had asked solemnly.

"I'm going to ignore that silly question and give you the relevant data," Chase said. "You gave me the name of Enterprise Realty, is that correct?"

"Yes, that's them."

"Then yes, the data I'm giving you is correct. Enterprise Realty isn't just real estate they do land development as well. Enterprise has a bad reputation because they have the reputation of being ambulance chasers."

"Ambulance chasers?"

"Yes, it means that they read the obituaries and hang out at hospitals. When people with real estate go in, they start making a pitch to get the land for cheap by trying to give the families money or by promising them they won't have to go to court if they sign over everything to them."

"You still think they are getting updates from within, though?"

Lionel snorted. "I don't think about betrayal. I know when it's happening. I'm telling you, you have a leak in your organization. Their timing is just too good, and it matches your need too well."

Michael took a deep breath and remembered he had to return to the kids, lunch was almost over. As Michael went out to the kids without Cora, he thought, *we are definitely going to make an adjustment to the contract.*

Cora wished she had taken the time to wear clothes that were a little more business orientated. Instead, she had on her black jeans and a light blue top. Melinda was in similar garb except that she had on a white shirt. The both of them were in a coffee bar trying to call Ben since he wasn't in his office and no one seemed to have an idea of his whereabouts.

"He's not answering?" Cora asked.

Melinda sighed and looked around. "He's been hard to catch lately."

"Okay, let's start at the beginning. How do the warrants usually come?" Cora asked calmly.

Melinda's jaw tightened, and she blew out a breath. "They are pinned to the door or left on my desk."

"Left on your desk?" Cora looked at Melinda's face. "You mean someone takes it off of the door, or do you mean they get access to the main cabin and leave it there?"

Melinda's frightened expression was all the answer Cora needed.

"So we are not just getting the warrants, they are being delivered by someone on the camp," Cora said, floored by the discovery. "What does Veronica say to that? I'm sure she has a suspicion."

Cora looked at Melinda, who was slumped in her chair with her eyes closed.

"Oh my goodness, we haven't told Veronica."

Melinda nodded sadly. "I haven't. Veronica gave this to me to handle. I went to Ben to help me," she whispered.

Cora let the words sink in, and then she started to think about what other options she had. "Melinda, do you have any of the warrants? Or do you know where a copy of them might be?"

Melinda nodded. She pulled out her phone. "I have a picture of one, front and back. I send them to Ben before I send them to the lawyer person we used to have."

"Good, let me see one." As she looked at Melinda's phone, Cora tried to think herself out of this predicament.

"I need your help, Cora."

"I wish people would come to me with a problem before it's critical. Give me a few moments, I'm almost done reading."

By the time she had finished reading the warrant and who issued it, Cora's resolve was clear. "Okay, I have a plan."

Melinda frowned. "You have a lawyer?"

"No, I don't, but all of these are issued by the authority of Enterprise Realty."

Melissa nodded in confusion. "I know that."

"Maybe you didn't take the time to see the signature of a partner for Enterprise Realty?"

Melinda took the phone Cora was giving back, and she looked at the signature.

"Oh my goodness, I never even gave it a second look," Melinda said.

"So, it seems obvious to me what we have to do."

Melinda looked skeptical. "I'm listening."

"The first thing we have to do is go see the president of Enterprise Realty, Glory Danvers. We've got to tell her it's time to stop playing these games."

Melinda looked at Cora for a minute. "What is the point of us going to tell her anything? Why is she going to listen to us?"

"She's going to listen to us because I know what she really wants." Cora looked at her watch, and then she looked at Melinda.

"We need to go. I think Glory is a creature of habit, and we need to get to the city and catch her before she leaves. The trip to the city is going to take at least an hour, so we've got to get going."

Nineteen

It was time to face this lingering demon. Cora had included her doubts about Glory and Michael into her rationale on why it wouldn't work. Since Michael and she had been working on their relationship, Cora knew there was nothing going on between them, but this would be the first time Cora was actually in the same room with the woman she had thought would steal Michael from her since her break up with Michael.

During their separation, every time she had received a copy of a contract with Glory's signature, it was another nail in the coffin. Anyone who had seen Glory would believe that she had it all. When Cora looked at Glory, what she saw was a woman who had all of the attributes that she didn't have. Glory was statuesque, lean, and shapely. Glory knew how to socialize and laugh at all the right times. Where Glory was a social butterfly, Cora was a steady woman that didn't really stand out in a crowd.

When Cora had met Glory, she saw all the pretty things about Glory but she also had a sense that Glory was missing something. Cora remembered telling

Michael that Glory was a little too close and a little too needy. At the time, Michael had laughed it off, but as time went on, Cora could see Glory working her wiles on Michael.

The day she had walked in to find Glory hanging over Michael's shoulder, she knew what Glory wanted. Michael seemed oblivious to Glory's antics. After the tragedy, it seemed like Michael had gone to Glory for comfort and it just reinforced her insecurities. However, in hindsight, she could tell that the reason he wouldn't ever wind up staying in Glory's presence was that he was doing more business with her to get past the grief of their loss.

During the ride, Cora had to keep herself quiet so she wouldn't snap at Melinda, who was proving to be a chatterbox.

"How close you must have worked with Glory to know where her office is," Melinda said as they drove to Glory's office.

"It's not a matter of closeness like friends. Thalman Designs did a lot of work with Danvers Inc. She does paint art and other detail work in a building. While she's not the easiest person to work with, I will say she usually does the best quality work."

"You know I think it's very woman-to-woman for you to go there, but I'm not really sure how this is going to work?"

"I'm going to threaten her with Michael walking away," Cora explained.

"Michael?" Melinda said, confused. "You know I don't want to get into anyone's business, but it seems odd to say you'll tell Michael not to speak to her if she doesn't do what you say."

Cora smiled. "Not exactly. In the field of house building and renovation, the market is small. People make connections based on if you've worked with someone or not. While her realty business may be something she runs on the side; her design business is her main business. If Michael told everyone he wasn't working with Glory anymore, that would be enough speculation for everyone to say they won't work with her until Michael goes back. I'm hoping it won't come to that, but I have to allow for the fact that it could happen," Cora finished in a tired voice. She looked at the passing scenery as it was changing from the country landscape to the subtle signs of the city.

Melinda tsked as she drove. "I think you give her a lot more leeway than I would. I don't think anything will stop her. She seems like the type of person who would sacrifice everything to be right. Ben and I thought we had it all handled. How did it get away from us so fast?"

"You would be amazed at how many people don't recognize the severity of warrants. At least you tried to answer them with a lawyer."

Melinda sighed. "I was so wrong to think we could handle this."

"Hey, what's done is done. Don't think about what you did wrong. The truth of it is we all did business with Danvers. We didn't know what that meant or what kind of person she was. You did all you could do with what you knew and what you had. You need to be content with that and let it go."

When they arrived at Glory's office, it was a reminder of who Glory was. The office was done in pastels and the furniture was done in rich woods. The art was some sort of expressionistic art where you couldn't tell what the picture was. The office was in a tall, shiny building, and the people who worked there looked picture perfect. When they stepped off of the elevator, a picture-perfect young lady sat at the desk.

Melinda murmured behind her. "We didn't call. She may not be in."

"She's in. The only question is, will we have to wait or not?"

The young lady flashed a smile that was so white Cora wanted to shield her eyes.

"How can I assist you?" Then as she got a better look at Cora, the young lady's smile tightened so much Cora was sure she would pull something on her face. "Hello, Ms.?"

Cora leaned on the desk. "Unless you know something that I don't, it's still Mrs. Thalman, I kept the name. Is Glory in?"

The young lady swallowed and then straightened her already stiff-as-a-board back.

"I'm sorry, Ms. Danvers is busy today, but if you leave your name and a number I can get back to you, or I can schedule—"

Cora nodded for about a minute and then just walked by the secretary.

"Don't worry, I'm sure she'll want me to interrupt now rather than deal with the spill-out later," Cora said. Cora could hear the outraged gasp from the secretary and the scampering of Melinda following behind her.

Glory was sitting on the edge of her desk looking at her hand as she talked on the phone. She didn't seem to be involved in the phone call as much as she was involved in the polish on her hands. Cora cleared her throat and Glory turned around to face her with a hint of amusement on her face. When Glory looked around Cora and saw Melinda, her expression turned to delight. While nothing but concern was in her voice, she ended the conversation.

"You know, Steven, you've given me a lot to think about. I want to make sure I give you the best option. Let me mull this over for a little while, and then we can meet up, say later tonight around six?a I know I'll have a complete package ready for you that will bring out the designs you've created."

Glory hung up the phone and then took a seat.

"Well, I have to say I was unaware that this was going to be a reunion day. How did I get so lucky to see some old business partners and new business partners in the same day?"

Cora looked at Glory, and all of a sudden, she didn't look as awe-inspiring as she once did.

"I think referring to me as a partner is a misnomer, but I can see how you might have given that name to yourself. I don't think this is a reunion day as much as it is a rectification day. I think we need to talk about the contracts that you have with Thalman as well as the warrants you've been sending to the camp under the business name Enterprise Realty."

Glory covered her mouth with her hand and her eyes grew wide. Her face was filled with glee.

"I can see we've already gathered the troops. When I look at you all, I can see how you might be a little miffed, but don't despair, if you will all just comply. I'm sure it will all be better." Glory angled her head and looked at Melinda. "I don't know why you're here. I sent you plenty of notices about my intent," she said slyly. "I think that the both of you are just upset."

Melinda stood her ground. "I don't understand what it is that you want. We're a camp for goodness' sake. You don't need the money, so what is it?"

"Look, I'm offering you a good deal. I want you to move so I can make a profit on the land. It's so silly to waste the land in this way. Do you think a bunch of foster kids will really notice if it's one place or another?"

Cora looked at Glory and in that moment, she felt free. Free from the worry of Glory and Michael. Free from the concern that she wouldn't measure up to Glory. More importantly, she felt free from the insecurity that maybe Michael would leave her for another woman. In her head, she had made Glory the ideal woman who would one day come and take Michael away from her.

"We won't be moving, Glory," Cora said calmly. "This isn't going to go the way you think it is. At one time, we were at least social. We can still correct whatever is between us without having it go any further."

"Have you by chance, bought into that idea of visualizations? If you did, I think you should give it up." Glory said sadly. "Whatever we had is gone. I don't know why Michael decided to stay with you. He would have been happier with me."

"Michael would have never gone with you Glory. He's an amazing man. He's a bit too giving, but that's Michael," Cora said.

Glory snickered. "Do you really believe that? When the two of you separated who did he run to? I know men like Michael; they can't stand to be alone. I put in the time with Thalman's Designs, and all I ever got was the runoff. I thought as we worked together that I'd get more from our deals. You all used me and then went on to promote yourselves without including me."

Cora braced herself for this moment she didn't want to have with Glory.

"I think it's time we put all of our cards on the table. I won't argue with you over the past. I think you should know that if you don't stop the warrants and sign the revised contracts that I've sent to you regarding Thalman, I'll have Michael break the business relationship. Publicly."

Glory hesitated, but her smile didn't falter. The look in her eyes wasn't as sure as it had been.

"Michael wouldn't do that to me. I've been there when you weren't. You can't prove I've done anything malicious either. I know you've been on that camp with him, but at the end of the day, he'll remember I was here for him."

"Think about what you want—what you're willing to risk—but I wanted to give you the opportunity to do the right thing."

"If the right thing had been done we wouldn't be here. By the time I'm done, everyone will see the right thing, and I'll be the one who'll call the shots with my fair share."

"We're done," Cora said. "You can expect to hear from Michael. I hope you find what you're looking for Glory."

"Whatever. Do whatever you want. It won't change a thing," Glory said in a high pitch tone. Cora was almost to the door when she heard Glory call her name.

"Cora!"

"Yes, Glory?"

"You think it'll work out but it never does. Men come and go and when you've washed up, then they forget you. It's the way of things."

Cora smiled. "It doesn't have to be. When you find the right person, it will be different. I hope you find someone special to show you that."

Cora and Melinda left Glory's office. When they got to the bottom floor, Melinda spoke.

"I don't think she was all that convinced," Melinda said as she went to the car.

"Probably not, but I had to give her the chance."

"If you knew she wouldn't take your suggestion, why did we come? More importantly, what do we do now?"

"Well, what we do now isn't an issue because there's only one choice. I am going to do what I said I would. I'll have to tell Michael."

Melinda stopped and looked horrified at Cora.

"Do you really think Michael will do that?"

Cora smiled. "He won't be happy but I'm sure once I talk to him, he'll understand, and it will be fine."

Melinda was mumbling all the way to the car.

Cora got in and waited until Melinda was on her way to the camp.

"It's not as bad as you think, Melinda. This will all work out."

"I hope so because right now, I don't see it, but if you do, I'll follow it."

The only thing Cora could think about was she couldn't wait to get back to the camp so she could meditate the stress away.

Twenty

Melinda drove them back and then she wanted to talk. It was later than she had expected, but the weather had held up today, and the evening wasn't as chilly as it had been. It was the end of the week, and frankly, the last two weeks had been more excitement than she had thought she would be signing up for. Cora couldn't even process that there was still another week left to the camp.

She had dressed in her comfy yoga pants, and she pulled out a blanket to put on the grass out front. She knew at some point she was going to have to talk to Michael. She wasn't sure how she was going to bring it up.

Cora knew Michael. He would be outraged and then sad about Glory's situation. At one time, she would have misinterpreted his sadness for her as some type of affection, but she knew now that Michael was just that kind.

She was sitting cross-legged on the blanket and taking deep breaths, relaxing into her pose. It was all going to work out just fine. Especially now that they had a contract and things were all out in the open, life would be easier after the initial shock. She was taking a second deep breath when her whole body got an abrupt jolt when she heard Michael's voice.

"I'm feeling so confused right now Cora." He walked slowly toward her. "On the one hand, I don't want there to be anything wrong with you, but if there was something wrong, at least that would have been an uncontrollable event. However, my gut is telling me that you are in perfect shape and the problem is that something happened, and you decided to dart off to try and handle it yourself. Tell me which one of these options is closest to the truth?" Michael asked in a low voice.

Cora's whole body was on alert. She had been through too much, faced and conquered too many old demons today, to back down to what she perceived to be a challenge to her abilities.

"Did you get the message from Evan?" Cora asked.

"Yes," he bit out.

"Well, then you received all of the message and warning that I could have possibly given any other reasonable adult. Now, if you would be so kind as to step back because your negative energy is disturbing me."

"I'd like to talk to you," he said.

"I'd like to talk to you as well, but maybe now is not the time. I don't think we could do anything productive." She heard Michael pacing and then letting out a big sigh.

"Fine, when you are ready to be responsible, let me know."

Cora opened her eyes and gripped her knees to stop herself from jumping up and launching herself at his back.

"Excuse me?"

Michael looked over his shoulder. "Oh, I'm sorry, are you ready to talk?"

"I can't believe you are acting so childish. Since this can't wait, even though it is beyond late, let's talk. What do you want to know?"

"Where were you today? I saw you last night and then this morning you were gone. I got some news on the realty company and you were gone. I left messages for you, and I sent you texts."

"I was out and I forgot my charger so I didn't have time to go through my messages. I know we are together. I get that, but just because we're together doesn't mean I'm suddenly, not an adult."

"We have a contract Cora. It says we talk to each other. I hope that even without the contract, neither one of us would just leave without notice."

"I left a notice, and you are being unreasonable. What is it? Why are you pushing for this fight? I've been through enough today."

"Just what have you been through?"

Cora was about to go on about Glory, and then she stopped. This was not the way she wanted to have this conversation.

"You are messing it all up!"

"What can I be messing up? I don't know anything."

"Michael, let it go, alright. Just let it go," she said as she got to her feet and went to her cabin. Her foot was on the first step when she heard his small voice.

"I was worried about you, Cora. I was scared, and I couldn't find you."

It was so low she almost couldn't hear him. When the words sank in, she grabbed the rail of the steps, and she let out a deep breath before turning around.

"You will be the death of me. Why were you scared? You just saw me last night." When she saw him, her anger shifted to concern. Whatever it was, she could tell Michael was really scared.

"I found out about the realty company, they have a bad reputation. I know Glory is working with them, but I think she's gotten herself in deep this time. When you disappeared, I went into the main cabin and found a warrant on Melinda's desk. I know you, Cora. You champion the underdog in a second with no concern for your own hide."

"I want to talk about it, but not now, okay? I need you to trust me Michael. I'm fine, you can see for yourself. Let's call a truce. Come in for coffee and tell me about the kids."

They made it into the kitchen, where they poured themselves two cups of instant coffee.

"How was today?"

"Peter was a little distracted, but we talked, and he seemed okay."

"He has a lot on his mind now," Cora said.

"Yeah, I told him to take some time and think things through. News came from the caseworker that it looks like things aren't doing so well for their foster parents. I wanted to talk to you about it."

"About us being their next foster parents? Michael, that is a huge step. Are we ready for that?"

Michael ran a hand through his hair. "I don't think we are ready for a baby. I think Peter and Lili are more our speed."

"And our lifestyle? How often are you home?"

Michael looked into his cup. "I can change my schedule. The good and the bad news is that they are almost of age. If they want to be with us, we can help them go to school and then they won't be home all the time. If they decide it was good and now they're ready to fly off to vocational, they'll leave the house again. I think the both of us are at points in our lives when we can make our own schedules."

Cora took a sip of her coffee. "It's true, neither one of us are hurting for money. We could offer them a good life."

Michael smiled. "Besides, I think after talking with Peter. I can do this. We can do this," he said confidently.

Cora looked at him and swallowed. "I am open to fostering because there is a need, and I have grown attached to them while we've been here. We have to do what's best for them, and it's got to be their choice, agreed?"

"We've got this!"

Cora was about to say something to Michael's optimistic cheer when someone knocked on her door.

"I guess the camp is up," she murmured. When she opened the door, Evan was on the other side. Instead of his smiling, hungry self, his face was serious, and seeing him like that put Cora on alert.

"What's wrong?" she asked.

"Is Michael with you?"

Michael came up behind her and put his hand around her waist. Whatever Evan had to say, Cora thought she might really need the hand.

"I just got the call. Peter has been arrested."

When Michael walked into the police station, Peter's eyes were darting back and forth. He was alone on the police bench, hunched over and tapping his feet in what appeared to be nervousness. All the anger that Michael had been feeling on the drive over washed away. Michael thought back to how moments ago he had told Cora they could do this. Looking at Peter, he thought back to what Cora said. Whatever they did had to be what was in the best interest of the children.

Peter was sitting on a bench, not a cell. Michael was glad that he had convinced Cora not to come. She said she was going to be strong, but he could imagine her running to Peter and holding him close, unintentionally embarrassing him in what was already a bad situation for him.

This is what it would be like to have Peter as his own. For the good times and the not-so-good times. This would also be a part of Cora's life with Lili. Had he waited too long? Was he still in good enough shape to put the fear of a father into a potential suitor who came to the door to take Lili out? He had always planned on having a family with Cora. She was the perfect mother.

Peter looked up and met his gaze, and the boy's body relaxed, his foot-tapping stopped, and Michael could see him straining to see if he had come alone. Michael waved to one of the cops who came to the counter.

The officer nodded back.

"I'm here for the young man on the bench, Peter. Can you tell me what he was picked up for?"

"He didn't do anything wrong. We found him on the side of the highway on a skateboard. We asked him what he was doing, and he said he was thinking. When we asked him where he lived and where his parents were, he said he had no home and no parents. At that point, we couldn't leave him; it was a safety issue for him."

"He's right. I'm his counselor at the foster camp on 32."

The officer smiled. "Oh, you mean Veronica's place?"

Michael nodded. "Yes, I'm Michael Thalman."

The officer gave him a good look. "You're going to have to sign papers, and then I can let him go with you."

Michael went to Peter, who stood up as he approached.

"Are Cora and Lili in the car?" Peter asked as he bent down and pulled his board from under the seat.

"As far as I know, no one has told Lili, and Cora is back at the camp counting the seconds before we return. I didn't think you would want me to bring her until she had time to calm down. We'll have to make a pit stop so she can do all that hugging before you sleep, but it won't be a public display," Michael said with a grin.

Peter let out a sigh and looked at Michael. "Thanks for coming."

"Did you doubt it?"

Peter shrugged. "Things happen."

The officer came, and Michael signed Peter out. "You ready?"

"More than."

When they left the station and got into the jeep, Peter sat in the front and looked at Michael with a raised eyebrow.

"It's Evan's."

"Ahh," Peter said. After the car had been moving a minute, Peter said, "I didn't do anything."

"You just got arrested. Most people will consider that a feat."

Peter leaned back and sighed. "Does this mean I'm getting kicked out of the camp?"

"No."

"Well, what's going to happen?"

"Well, tonight, you are going to hug Cora and let her kiss your cheek. Tomorrow we will talk again. I know I told you to think, but I'm sure I didn't tell you to talk back when a cop asks you questions."

"I didn't know what to do. I knew I wasn't supposed to be out late, but I think the best when I'm on my board. I got on, and I found out I was further than I thought. I was on my way back when the cop showed up."

"Think things through. It's a lesson you are never too old to learn," Michael said solemnly.

"When did you learn that?" Peter asked.

They stopped at a light, and Michael looked over at Peter and smiled. "It turns out I'm still learning it."

Twenty-one

Michael was in front of Cora's cabin with sweets and coffee. It had only been a couple of hours since he last saw her. When she saw Peter, she opened her arms and hugged him. She couldn't really speak, and she was blinking a lot. When she pulled back from his arms, there were tears on both of their faces. He heard Peter whisper I'm sorry, and she pulled him into her arms again.

Early the next morning Michael had gone into town to get some danishes. He knew her favorite was cinnamon, and when he saw the buns fresh out of the oven, he asked for four to put in the box. Then he stopped and picked up some coffee, he figured he had what he needed to make amends.

He'd been up all night reading on what classes for foster parents to take. He looked at the possible challenges they could face, not knowing everything about Peter and Lili. The road could be challenging, and they made it sound like last night's encounter with the police was mild. Foster parents had to be ever vigilant to see the signals that children could be giving about their insecurities or problems.

As if she knew he was outside, the door opened, and Cora looked at him. A smile bloomed on her face. She was in her yoga pants and a tank top. He could see her lean body as the morning breeze hugged her legs.

"I see someone is here early, and it's not even a camp day," she said.

"I brought offerings, coffee, and cinnamon buns."

She leaned against her door and gave him a raised eyebrow. "I can see you wanted to make sure you had my attention."

"I did want your attention but recently someone commented that my delivery on getting a person's attention shouldn't make me treat them like a child. This time I wanted to do it the right way. It's funny, someone reminded me I needed to think things through."

"Well, let me commend you on your delivery," then the smile fell from her face, "but I can't accept it if this is about Peter and Lili."

Michael looked in each bag and then up at Cora. "I assure you Peter and Lili are not in these bags."

"Michael, I was a wreck last night. I couldn't even have a cohesive conversation on what went wrong. I was so happy that he was safe that all I could do was hug him and cry. I don't think I can do this," she told him in a low voice.

"Coffee or the Cinnamon?"

She pushed away from the frame. "No, parenting." She looked over Michael's shoulder and then looked him in the eye. "I don't think I'd be any good at being a foster parent with you."

Michael thought he was coming here to prove that he could learn, and now that he was here, he found out that Cora was thinking she had done something wrong. "Cora, it's early in the morning, and you've always thought quicker than me. Let's go over this. What do you think the problem is here?"

"First, he went to you to talk. I'm fine with that, he's a boy. When he came back last night, I had no words. You two looked like you were best buds, but I was a sore thumb. I think you might need a better partner to be a foster parent. I didn't do anything, and you seemed to know exactly what to say."

"I'm going to tell you a secret, and it's going to explain last night to you, so you don't feel bad."

Cora stood with her arms over her chest. "I don't think you can do that, but okay."

"Cora, once upon a time, I was a teenage boy. I didn't listen to my family, and when I got in trouble, my whole family came to get me. It was by far one of the most embarrassing moments of my life. The football team never let me live it down that my mom was crying, and my dad had decided that he would explain in detail what my punishment was going to be while we were in public. I never forgot that, and I decided I'd never do that to a kid. You didn't miss anything; I just have the advantage of having already been a teenage boy."

They both laughed, and then she cleared her throat. "I'm scared Michael."

"I know. I'm scared when I read the books on it, but when I think about us doing it together, it doesn't seem so scary."

She let out a breath and then looked at the bags in his hands. "So how many cinnamons are in there?"

He laughed. "Hopefully enough to get me entry."

She stepped aside and he took the coffee and danishes to the kitchen. Cora got plates and mugs, and then they both sat down, took a Danish apiece, and began to eat.

"Cinnamon," she moaned. "I'm so glad you remembered."

Michael looked at her biting into the Danish with her eyes closed, and he wondered if she knew how good she looked. This was Cora. She was all in, all the time. If she was happy, it was all there. If she was sad, it was all there as well.

"You know one of the main things we have to make sure of is that we keep our time and our relationship healthy. When kids come into the picture—foster children or not—it seems like adults forget they have needs as well."

"Do we need to add to the contract?" Cora asked as she licked her fingers.

"Maybe, but I want to test the amendment before I add it to the contract. He stood and pulled Cora to her feet as well.

"What is this amendment that you need to test?" she said, smirking, looking at him.

"I think that every morning we should make sure we kiss, to remember us."

"Every morning? I have a pretty good memory," she joked.

"Well, the point is if we do it every morning, later we won't have to admit we're getting old and have change schedules from once a week to every day because we're forgetting. We'll keep it every day, and we'll be fine."

"That was a horrible explanation," she chuckled.

"I'm anxious. I'll come up with something better later."

Then he lowered his head to hers and kissed her. Just when he wrapped his arms around Cora and pulled her close. Just when he was about to deepen the kiss, someone knocked at the door.

Michael groaned. "It can't be, I came early, and there's no camp."

Cora moved out of his arms and went to open the door. "Hey Cora, is Michael here?"

"Of course Evan…"

Michael shook his head. "This better be important."

"Yeah, Peter was looking for you," Evan said.

Cora smiled. "I guess I'll see you later."

Twenty-two

Michael went to Melinda's cabin. He rang the doorbell and waited for her to answer. When she saw who was at the door, she didn't open the door all the way. Instead, she peered at him like a cat ready to run.

"Michael."

"I think we should discuss this inside because I don't think you want anyone to hear what I have to say."

Melinda stepped back and opened the door. "I want you to know that I don't regret what I did."

"Yeah, I didn't think you would regret it, but I have to ask why? We see each other often enough."

"I do see you. I see you going to get ready for Cora. I see you passing by to do something for Veronica. I see you doing and going a lot of places, but have you ever asked yourself how often we talk?"

"So because we're not social, you hold on to the warrants, and don't tell me?"

"I told Ben, and we were trying to handle it."

"So I hear. When the lawyer didn't work, why didn't you come then?"

Melinda sat down on her brown couch and sighed. "I kept hoping it would work out, and maybe the work the lawyer would figure it out. I mean, Ben and I had to pay the lawyer a lot of money to get motions passed to stop the warrants for a while. Then they just started up again."

"How much money are we talking about?"

"It was about ten thousand each."

Michael whistled. "I guess the camp pays well."

Melinda waved him off. "It wasn't a lift for me, but I know it hit Ben hard. When the price tag came up, he said he didn't want to go to Veronica. If the lawyer could address it, then we wouldn't have to worry. I was able to get my share, but I know it took him longer."

Michael sat across from Melinda, trying to contain his frustration. "Did anyone else know about the warrants? Evan?"

"We couldn't tell him. Evan would have told you right away," she said, exasperated. "The two of you are thick as thieves. Besides, I'm of the firm belief that Evan would tell anything for food. Besides, after we started paying a lawyer, I really thought the problem would go away."

"Funny to me though that when Cora was told she had to run off and try to take care of your problem."

Melinda fell back against the couch. "That was an accident. In fact, it happened so fast that I can't really recall which one happened first or second. It seemed like I had been going over the issues at camp and then I hit one of those moments when I knew I couldn't do it anymore and—"

"She just happened to be there?"

Melinda sat up and stared at Michael, tense with anger. "Listen, I admit that I was getting tired of carrying it on my shoulders. Ben is nice, but he isn't really helpful when it comes to these types of things. It was a relief to talk to someone. However, I would have never guessed in a million years that when I told her, she would want to go right away to see Glory."

Michael sighed. "I know. You wouldn't know that, but I know that's how Cora is. She wouldn't let a friend stay in trouble. She's not that kind of person. My problem is when she went to see Glory that she made herself a potential target."

"Target?"

"Real estate is big business, and I need to keep Cora safe."

Melinda stared at Michael and then started shaking her head. "You know Michael, when you started this whole adventure, and you said you wanted to get Cora back, I really thought that it was so romantic. I didn't think it was appropriate in the camp, but still romantic. Now that I know Cora a little better. I think that maybe you and Cora aren't so great a match."

"What?"

Melinda frowned. "Cora is so helpful and planned and organized. I mean, I know that she ran off with me to Glory's, but she doesn't let problems stay, and she's so attentive. Those are not things I would associate with you, Michael. Maybe you should consider that you're not the best thing for her?"

"You're too late. I know I'm not good enough, but I'm working on it, and she won't find another who will love her more. But enough, we can sit here all day and go over how unworthy I am of Cora. I need all of the warrants."

"What are you going to do?"

Michael stood up. "I'm going to look at all of the information and give it to a friend of mine. Then I'll make sure I fix this issue."

Melinda looked amazed. "You really are going to fix this, aren't you?"

"Yes."

Melinda looked a little livelier. "She said you would. She said that you'd do the right thing. Maybe she does know what she's getting into."

Michael dreaded what was to come. He made the drive to the city and thought about how it would go when he made it to Danvers' office. When he got off the elevator, the young lady at the desk smiled and asked, "How may I help you?"

"You can't help me. In fact, this is something I should have addressed much earlier." Michael walked past the slack-jawed girl, opened the door to Glory's office and closed it behind him. Then locked it.

Glory Danvers was sitting at her desk on the phone. As soon as she saw him, she gave him a large smile, and her voice, which was smooth as butter, continued.

"I've been reviewing the documents for the last couple of days. I've personally dedicated the time to research it from every angle. I wanted to make sure it was airtight before I presented it to my top three clients. I might be able to hold them off for a little while longer…hold on for a moment." Glory pushed a button on her phone. "Michael, did I miss an appointment?"

"I've got no appointment. I'm here about Cora."

Glory's whole countenance fell, and the smiling woman who was sitting at the desk turned into a hard businesswoman.

"If you're here about her, go to the girl at the front and set something up. I don't have time now."

He walked up to her desk and sat down in the chair in front of her. "I think you need to make time Glory. This won't hold, and I'd rather have it now than let our lawyers have it."

Glory's eyes had narrowed, and if it had been possible, she would have had flames shooting out of them. "You're coming in here as an avenging angel for Cora? Do you even want to hear what happened, or has she wrapped you around her finger so much the truth doesn't matter?"

"Wow, I can't believe I was as blind as I was for so long. I heard the truth, and I have a truth to deliver of my own. You need to tell your lawyers and your friends in Enterprise Realty to stop harassing Veronica. All of the warrants have been answered, and there are a slew of counter warrants being issued to all the primary owners of Enterprise. I suspect that means you'll be receiving a warrant or two."

"You think you have that kind of clout to tell me what to do Michael?"

He stood up and smiled. "To be honest, after I finished getting all of the information back on what you were doing, I realized I'm not the one who could move your business one way or another. As it turns out though, I have a friend. My friend would matter in your world."

"Really?" she said smugly.

"Really Glory. Lionel Chase would vouch for me, and he would put out the word that if you want to work with him, they can't work with Enterprise. The choice is yours, like it's always been."

He walked to the door and unlocked it. As he pulled it open, he heard Glory ask.

"Is she worth it?"

He looked over his shoulder and nodded at her. "This, and so much more. I'll see you around Glory…or not."

Twenty-three

Michael's mornings were filled with joy knowing he was going to be with Cora. Today he had been summoned to see Veronica with Cora. As he went to the door, Ben opened it. Ben had an accusing glare on his face.

"I can't believe it."

"Believe what?"

"You and Cora are really getting together?"

"That was the goal all along," Michael said.

Ben shook his head. "I had hoped the girl would be smarter and wouldn't fall for your charms. Things come so easy for you Michael, while the rest of us work our—"

Any chance for him to respond was cut off as Cora arrived a bit breathless behind him.

"Oh dear, I hope I'm not too late," Cora said as she kept her smile and looked at him and Ben.

Michael stepped aside as Cora went in and then looked over his shoulder at Ben. "Your opinion was noted. Thankfully, Cora doesn't feel that way." With that, he closed the door and went into the room with the two women who held a special place in his heart, for different reasons.

When he walked into the room, instead of the warm atmosphere he was used to, he found Cora sitting straight-backed in a chair and Veronica on the other side of the desk she almost never sat at. He came in and put a chair next to Cora.

Veronica gave him a raised eyebrow and continued the conversation it appeared he had walked into the middle of.

"I'm glad you could find your way here. I was just telling Cora how I like to be kept informed of what goes on at the camp. Part of the reason I pick each person has to do with the fact that I know I can trust them."

"Nothing is going to happen to the camp, Veronica. If there was a problem that couldn't be handled, you'd be told."

"Ah, and maybe that is where the understanding you have is flawed. I don't want to know of things when they've gotten so out of hand you can no longer find an answer for it. I want to be kept abreast of when things go on here *as they are occurring*. Is there anything that is occurring that you'd like to speak on?"

"Not really," Michael said.

"Let's try again," Veronica demanded. "I want to know about lawyers inquiring into the camp and maybe about warrants that just seem to manifest out of nowhere."

Cora was stock-still and looked anxiously at Michael. "Any of those kinds of things would be action items that Michael would address immediately."

Michael sat back and let Cora speak. The set in Veronica's jaw, and the way she enunciated every syllable were all signs of her annoyance. When he realized that Cora couldn't pick up on the signs he saw in Veronica because she hadn't known Veronica as long as he had, he stepped in.

"We had all of those problems and more. We've addressed the problem, and it's been put to rest."

Veronica turned her shrewd glance on him. "You're sure? My lawyers have assured me that all of the legal issues have been addressed. However, in the same breath, they all told me that not one but both of you went to see Danvers. That suggests to me that maybe there is some more business that needs to be addressed."

Michael kept his gaze on Veronica when he replied. "It was just clean up. I wanted to make sure there were no more flare-ups of this kind."

"Good." Veronica looked at Cora. "I want to thank you for coming so early. I know you usually do your meditation in the morning. If you don't mind, I'd like to talk to Michael."

Cora nodded and then gave a small smile to Michael. "Michael, I'll see you later." She looked between Veronica and Michael before exiting the room.

"I'm sure Veronica isn't going to mame me. I'll see you later."

"Veronica," Cora said with a nod.

"Again, thank you for making the time."

Michael watched Veronica watch Cora leaving and knew his clock was ticking. He had seen the responses to the warrants, and it wasn't from Melinda and Ben's lawyers. Every one of the orders, rebuttals, and even new warrants that were going out were all signed by Veronica herself. Veronica was never out of the loop she was just waiting for them to come to her.

When the door was closed, she focused on him like a laser.

"So, I see that the two of you are back together? The police station called and told me that you picked up Peter as well."

"I didn't know how well-informed you were."

"Young man, I shouldn't need to be that informed to know what is going on in my own camp. We have rules, Michael, and you are running amok as if we had never even talked. Cora is an amazing woman with great compassion. I'm concerned that your impulsiveness could be detrimental to a kind shoulder like hers."

"Everyone is real happy to let me know that I'm not the right person for Cora. I want you all to remember that Cora is a grown woman." He got up to leave.

Veronica stood up. "I won't allow anyone to keep me in the dark about what's going on in my own camp because people think it's too much for an old woman, and I won't be a part of a plan to get you a ready made family—no matter how innocent it seems—that will wind up hurting Cora."

Michael smiled as he opened the door. "Veronica, did any of you think about me?"

"Michael?"

Michael didn't stop. Instead, he kept going out the door and even saw Ben outside the cabin looking as sour as he felt. He knew what he needed and where she was.

Michael had liberated Evan's Jeep. When he was leaving, the only thing Evan said was that if he was going to get food, don't forget to bring him something back. He hadn't really expected Cora to meditate after that dismissal from Veronica, but true to form, she was sitting on her steps when he drove by.

"I need a friend."

Cora smiled and walked over to the jeep. "You're in luck. I happen to be feeling really friendly."

They both laughed as she got in and then he drove away. He drove down the highway until they reached a side route where he knew of a little diner. When they walked into the diner, everyone stopped. They weren't dressed any differently, but it was their luck that they came to the diner on the day that a seniors' party was going on, so they were the kids in the diner.

The waitress came up to them and smiled. "You two aren't from around here, are you?"

Michael smiled. "What gave it away?"

The waitress chuckled. "Every third Saturday is seniors' day. We don't put up a sign anymore because everyone knows, and it's so rare that we get outsiders. It's no problem. I'll seat you two on the side."

"We won't be long. We're just here for coffee and a danish at best."

"No problem, just wave, and one of us will come over. The seniors have rented out the whole diner and coffee, and Danish are on the menu. When you see a waitress come by you can take it from the platter. I'll let them know you're here."

"No, really we couldn't impose," Cora said.

The waitress waved them off. "It's more hassle for us to try to track you while we are working with the special members here. So, enjoy."

They found a booth and slid in across from one another. An older man came over and smiled. He leaned down and patted Michael on the shoulder before whispering loudly. "Don't mess it up."

When he left the both of them laughed.

"Okay, spill it. What did Veronica say?" Cora asked.

"It was nothing that I didn't expect. It was the fact that she knew all along, and we were wasting our time trying to do something without her knowing."

"Then why were you upset?"

Michael cocked his head to the side. "Was I?"

Cora shrugged away his question. "That was a silly question. I know you, Michael."

He leaned over and put her hands between his. "You know what, you do know me."

"So are you going to tell me or—?"

"Or I've already forgotten it. I don't want to talk about the camp. I want to tell you something that I think is very important."

Cora sat up and nodded. "Okay," she said cautiously.

"I think you are beautiful."

Cora smiled and looked away. "Okay, I thought we were going to have a serious conversation."

"You don't think that's important?"

"I mean it's not that it's not important but—"

"You know I never liked the word "but. I had an English teacher who explained to me that when a person used the word "but" it really meant forget everything I said before the word "but" only what I'm going to say is true or matters.

Cora laughed. "No—"

"So, I think you are beautiful. It's my opinion, so it's true for me. Also, I want you to know that I respect you. You are always upfront about what you can and can't do. I never realized how much I depended on it."

"I know this is going to sound wrong and probably not in the moment, are you okay?"

Michael smarted. "Wow, Cora, am I that bad? Is it so rare that I compliment you?"

Cora shrugged. "I know how you feel, Michael."

"Even though you know, it must be different to hear it though, right?"

Cora smiled. "Yes, it is."

"I want you to know, that goes both ways."

Cora was about to take a drink, and then she choked after he finished talking.

"Oh, Michael. Do you need me to tell you that you are amazing? Do you need to hear that you're talented, or do you need to hear that while you are all of those things, the reason I love you is because you make me laugh, and the future looks brighter with you in it?"

He swallowed and brought her hands to his lips. He placed small kisses on each knuckle and then took a deep breath.

"I know how you feel about me as well, but I have to say that it doesn't hurt to hear you say it."

Then one of the waitresses came by with a platter. He sat back and watched Cora laugh as she looked at the different cinnamon desserts with delight. When she smiled at him, it felt right. There weren't any questions, he didn't have any doubts. He thought he'd be beyond happy when it was all clear, but now that he was here, he was scared.

He had just found out a new truth. When a man has everything he could dream of, he knows fear like he's never known.

Twenty-four

It had taken him a little while to pull it together, but everything had to be perfect, and he was only going to get one shot at it.

"Hello, my name is Carl and—"

Michael looked up from the menu. He looked at the waiter in front of him and wondered if this was a portent of how the evening was going to go. "I'm curious, Carl where is my hostess?"

Carl's smile fell and he looked over his shoulder. "I, well, what happened was I saw that you were here, and I didn't want you to wait, so I just came over to try and help. I mean you know we normally try to help each other out and—"

"Stop stammering, man. Do you have the specials for the day?"

"Y-yes, sir. They are—" the young man dug into his side pocket and pulled out a card.

"Listen, don't bother trying to read it to me. Just give me the card, and you can go."

"Of course," Carl said as he put the card on the table. Then Carl turned toward Cora.

She gave him an encouraging smile. "Thank you, Carl, for jumping in and trying to help."

"Of course, I'll go and find your hostess for you." Carl gave a quick look at Michael, as he was one stop away from running.

Cora cleared her throat to get Michael's attention. "He was just trying to help. Don't shoot him down; remember, we were all there at one time."

Michael looked at the retreating back of the waiter. "I made a simple request. It shouldn't have been so hard to do."

"Patience Michael, we're all not on board about taking orders from you."

Michael wanted to defend himself, but if he did, it would only extend the sour moment. He could feel the sweat forming on his back. He could do this. He just needed to get through the gauntlet, right?

When they had arrived, Cora had smiled at him and made him feel like he was a superhero. This was the same restaurant they went to on their second anniversary, kind of. It was the right address, but their restaurant had gone out of business. In its place was this restaurant. The owner had told him that all the staff had stayed on. They just renamed it.

When Michael looked at the surroundings, he could see that the interior had been upgraded. He hoped the food was as good as the prices suggested. Just when Michael was about to start a conversation with Cora, the hostess showed up. It was the woman who had served them before, in the old restaurant. She wasn't exactly what Michael thought she would be.

The woman walked over slowly. Her hair was in a bun, and had been recently colored brown but not well.

The roots were a deep brown, but the bun was a tint of green. The hostess also had on so much makeup he wasn't sure if she was trying to cover up something or going for the clown look. He shook his head and waited for the horror to unfold.

"Hello, dears. I hear you all wanted me to serve you."

Michael smiled. "You were one of the servers who served us when we came here before the renovation," he explained.

"Oh, you all from there. Yeah, I remember there were a lot of good people who would come then. The tips were so much better as well. Hmm, let me look at ya."

She reached out and pushed Michael's hair back away from his forehead. Michael heard Cora swallow a laugh.

"Hmm, I'm sorry I don't recall you, but you look like good people. I'm a little slower now but if you want, I can serve you."

Michael turned and smiled at the woman. "No, you don't have to serve us; I just wanted to see a familiar face."

"Well, that you have, or at least my face is familiar to you. Well, if you want anything, call out. I'm here."

Michael watched her walk away, and at that moment, it all seemed clear that this night was going to go downhill, and his life was about to be ruined. Then he felt Cora's hand on his.

"Babe? I think it's sweet. I think everything you've tried to do tonight is amazing, and no matter what happens, I want you to know I appreciate the effort you put in."

Michael wanted to leave and cut his losses. Maybe he could go to the men's room and cancel the rest of the evening. He wanted to get her to a place where he could ask her if she was ready to have a life with him. He wanted to ask her if they were strong enough to be a foster family. How did a man just ask a woman if she was ready to change everything in her life with the guy who messed it up last time?

He thought he had it all planned, but looking at how the plans were panning out, he was discouraged. He was about to speak when he looked at her across the table, but the words left his head as he watched her, enthralled.

She was the star that shone brighter than anything in the sky. She was his guiding light and his hope for tomorrow. She had on a blue dress that draped over one shoulder and ended in a slant showing off her well-toned legs. The fabric moved with her, making it seem like she was a wave in motion. When she stopped, the fabric gently hung on her curves. The dress didn't cling, but it played peekaboo with his imagination. It was as if she had stepped out from some unearthly fantasy place to accompany him.

She was the one.

Did she want to be the one?

"Michael?"

"I think maybe we need a change in plans. Maybe we need to—" Just when he was about to suggest that they leave, he saw Evan and the kids.

Cora leaned in and ran her fingers down his jaw. "Michael?"

"I was wrong. I should have done this differently." He sat back and waited for them to come over, just as they had practiced it.

Evan was in slacks. Peter had on black slacks with a

blue top, and Lili had on a white-and-blue polka dot dress.

"Hey, guys! Figure meeting you here," Evan said, with a smile on his face.

"Why not?" Michael grumbled. "The night has not been as smooth as I thought, but don't worry, I'm sure this will make it all better."

"Michael," Cora chided. She jumped up and opened her arms to the kids.

"Hey guys, I'm so glad you're here!" Michael watched as hugs and kisses were shared among all. Carl showed up again, looking at Michael cautiously when Evan said. "We'll be joining this party. Make sure to put it all on Michael Thalman's tab."

Michael looked up at a smiling Evan. "You were entirely too happy saying that."

Evan looked around the table. "I haven't eaten all day. This is going to be an amazing dinner, and I want to make sure that I get my fill."

Michael sat back and was resigned to the evening. He looked at everyone at the table. Cora was laughing. The children had smiles in their eyes. It was everything that he wanted it to be. Surely, this was proof enough that they were meant to be a family.

Then, as if it couldn't get any worse, Veronica showed up.

"Hello, I can see this is the place to be tonight."

Michael looked at her and then at Evan, who couldn't look him in the eye. "Evan, you too, brother?"

Evan finally looked at him and shrugged with his hands held out. "There is no force that can stand up to Veronica. As much as I like you, I want you to know that I had to tell her everything."

"Everything?"

Michael had been so busy thinking about the betrayal from Evan that he failed to notice that Cora and the kids had stopped talking and that they were all looking at him.

"Everything like what?" Cora asked.

Veronica cleared her throat. "Well, dear, I'm sure you must strongly suspect that we didn't all just show up here. We're here to make sure the right thing is done."

Michael looked around and shook his head. "I want you all to know that I am perfectly capable of having a conversation with Cora without your help!"

Peter grabbed some bread and snorted.

"Do you have something to say, little man?"

"I'm not saying anything. I'm just saying that the whole time I've been here, I haven't heard you say anything to her, and I'm just waiting, is all I'm saying."

Cora smiled.

Veronica followed up behind Peter. "I have to say the boy is right. I mean, I'll be gone by the time you say anything."

"What is being said?" asked Cora.

Michael looked at Cora. "Give me one moment." Then they turned back to the group. "I've got this. I've been here before, so I remember how to ask my wife to share forever with me."

"Do you?" Cora asked.

Michael turned and looked at her incredulously. "Really, Cora? If you side with them, then I'll have to believe it's true. I asked you to marry me once. I know how to do it."

"Is that what you're asking me, Michael?"

Michael looked around the table. All of them looked

at him expectantly, except Lili, who was urging him on with both of her hands and a smile. Finally, Lili mouthed, "you've got this."

Michael turned to Cora. "I'm not asking you if you want to simply marry me. I'm asking you if you want to raise a family with me? I'm asking you if you want to grow old with me? I'll be making mistakes left and right. I'm asking if you'll share the rest of my tomorrows with me?"

Veronica broke in. "I just want you to know, we all think it's a big risk with Michael. So if you want to say no, there's no reason to feel pushed or rushed."

Michael couldn't look away from Cora. It all came down to this. If she didn't think he was worth taking the risk, then he didn't even know what would happen.

She leaned over and kissed him on the cheek.

Was that the last kiss?

Cora turned to everyone at the table. "Would everyone please leave the table for a moment?"

They all looked worried. Michael was worried. When they were gone, she turned back to him.

She pulled him closer and framed his face with her hands. "You have to know what my answer would be."

She placed a kiss on the right side of his mouth.

"You are my best friend and partner in crime."

She leaned over and placed a kiss on the left side of his mouth. Her hands traced his jaw and went up until they were around his neck.

"I love you, and I'll love whatever children we are so blessed to get. I hope it's Lili and Peter, but even if it's not, I'll still be here. We will still be here to do our part."

Then she leaned in and stopped right before their lips touched.

"My answer is a resounding yes. Yes to the adventure of a lifetime. Yes to the foster kids, but most of all, yes to you, Michael Thalman."

The relief was so intense that he stood up and took her with him and then pulled her into his arms and kissed her until he couldn't tell where he stopped, and she began. He heard the clapping and felt Evan's strong pat on his back, but he didn't break the kiss. This was the beginning of them. He wasn't worried that Cora wouldn't remember what they had; now, they were going to make new memories.

Sign up to my newsletter to receive updates on new releases, sale promotions, and free books.

susanwarnerauthor.com